WILLIAM BELL

William Bell is an award-winning author whose books are published in the United States and Europe as well as Canada. A teacher of English, Bell taught in China for two years. He makes his home in Orillia, Ontario.

When he is not writing or teaching, Bell likes to travel, watch car-racing on television, and read other people's books.

ABSOLUTELY
INVINCIBLE

WILLIAM BELL

A GEMINI BOOK

Published in 1993 by
Stoddart Publishing Co. Limited
34 Lesmill Road
Toronto, Canada
M3B 2T6
(416) 445-3333

General Paperbacks edition published in 1991.

First published by Irwin Publishing Inc.
under the title *The Cripples' Club*.

Canadian Cataloguing in Publication Data

Bell, William, 1945–
[Cripples' club]
Absolutely invincible!

First published in 1988 under the title: The cripples' club.
"Gemini".
ISBN 0-7736-7411-X

I. Title.   II. Title: The cripples' club.

PS8553.E55A62 1993   jC813'.54   C93-095067-4
PZ7.B45Ab 1993

Cover Design: Brant Cowie/ArtPlus
Cover Illustration: Don Kilby
Calligraphy by Ting Xing Ye

Printed and bound in the United States of America

*Stoddart Publishing gratefully acknowledges the support of the
Canada Council, Ontario Ministry of Culture, Tourism, and
Recreation, Ontario Arts Council, and Ontario Publishing
Centre in the development of writing and publishing in Canada.*

This book is for my son, Brendan.

Zhèn zùo qǐ lái

Acknowledgments

I would like to thank John Pearce for his help and
encouragement in the writing of this book.
To a considerable extent, *Absolutely Invincible!*
was inspired by two of my former students, Shelley and Darin,
and by the late Terry Fox.

PART
ONE

1

I remember some things.

Bob and Mitzi, who take care of me. Where I live. *Shīfu* and my workouts at the gym. I can read now, and do some arithmetic.

And at night sometimes, the strange dream with the jungle and the storm and the voice that screams over broken teeth.

But inside my head shadows fall on empty spaces. Things that happen, words people say, faces, thoughts — all get lost. They disappear.

I am in a washroom at the school.

There is a big, half-circle sink with a mirror above it. I stare at the face in the mirror. Dark hair, dark eyes. The face is blank. Nothing to see there. Only shadows.

馬

Now I am in the wide hall. It is filled with light from the big glass doors. Across from where I stand against the wall is a door with a sign: OFFICE. The hall is filled with students talking in excited voices. Some wear sweaters with ELMWOOD COLLEGIATE printed on them. The students are colorfully dressed and happy. They come and go. They stand in groups, talking and laughing. There are no shadows on their bright faces. Sometimes a grownup walks past. Some students call out greetings and the grownups smile. They know who they are. Grownups always do.

Music comes from the ceiling. The hall is almost empty now. A man dressed in brown comes up. He is taller than me.

"George." He looks at my face. "Why aren't you in class? You're late."

I do not answer. I'm afraid. I don't know where to go and I don't want him to find that out.

"You're in the Special Class, aren't you, George?"

Now I remember. The Special Class. I picture in my mind how to get to the room. Fifty steps down the hall. The door is green and it has a small window.

"Come on," says the man. "I'll take you there."

In the class the woman is talking. She is standing at the front, holding a book. The students are restless, buzzing with secret talk, but I sit quietly at the back. Outside the window a cloud slowly crosses the sun and a shadow crawls across the desk, eating the light. My hands darken.

I can feel myself slipping into The Well. My fingers grip the edges of the desk. My teeth clench but it is no use. I am falling down, down, down.

The Well is a place filled with terror that swirls around

me like black smoke. Sometimes I hear hollow voices I do not recognize drumming against the stone walls of The Well, like fists. When I fall, I try to keep still. I never reach the bottom.

After a time, the smoke clears and light breaks through. I find myself on the outside again. Safe. For a while. Afterwards, my bones ache with tiredness and my head throbs.

"George?"

The smoke is gone now and I am in a classroom. My hands are folded on the desk. A thin woman with blonde hair and a book in her hand is standing near me. The others are gone.

I look up at her. I remember her face. She is kind, I think.

"George, did you understand the story?"

I keep silent. What story does she mean? I think I read a story last night before I fell asleep. Is that what she means? I look at the book in her hand. Her finger is pinched between the pages. Maybe the story is in there.

"The story was about a boy who made a vow, George. Can you tell me what the vow was?"

She smiles, but her voice doesn't. I know what she is trying to do, now. She wants to trap me.

"I have to go," I say, and I get up quickly. I must get away.

"George!" she calls after me. "It's all right! I just —"

But the door slams and she disappears.

I am in the gym, now. Outside the gym it is dark. The big windows along one wall reflect the lights in the ceiling and the people lined up in three rows. There are fifteen of us. Outside, Bob is waiting for me in the car. He keeps the inside light on for me.

Shīfu's shouts bounce off the walls of the gym. "One! Two! Three!" — up to ten, then, *"Hài!"*

I am wearing my white *Shàolín* suit. A blue belt is knotted at my waist. I punch the air with each count, and the cloth on my sleeve goes *snap!* with each punch. We practice blocks, then kicks. Sweat runs down my body.

I am safe here. My feet are bare. My suit is loose and feels . . . natural, right.

Now we are sparring. This part I like best. My partner is a tall woman with a brown belt. I do not remember her, but she is good — very fast and tricky. Her short brown hair is messy and strands of it stick to her wet forehead. We fight quietly, except for the *"Hài!"* we shout when we strike. We are not allowed to let the punches or kicks land but the good ones snap against the partner's suit.

My mind is calm here.

I like *Shīfu*. His face I always remember. He is different from the others. Dark hair, dark eyes, flat nose. He has yellow skin. He is bigger than me but not as big as Bob. He is kind. He teaches me to be strong. He teaches my body to defend, then strike, to move with power. I am strong here.

I never slip into The Well.

Mitzi is sitting on the edge of my bed. She has a small, thin body like me. Her hair is long and red and her skin is very white. Her eyes are bright, like the eyes of the sparrows that sit on the ledge outside my window.

Mitzi and I have just finished reading a story. She reads some, then I read some. Back and forth.

"Did you like that story, George?" she asks, closing the thick book.

Already the beginning of the story is slipping away into

the shadows.

"Yes, I liked it," I answer. Mitzi is happy when I remember things, so I try to please her.

"You know, George, your reading is excellent. You've learned very quickly since you came to Canada. And your accent is almost completely gone."

She smiles. She is pleased with me. I do not know what an accent is, but I say nothing.

"You learned quicker than anyone I know. You're very smart, George. You're a very intelligent guy."

"Thank you, Mitzi."

"I want you to believe that, George. The school put you in the Special Class with those other kids because they don't understand you. Bob and I are trying to change that. But it may take a while."

She lays the thick brown book on the comforter between us. The comforter is yellow and white, sun colors. The curtains in my room are the same colors. They shut the night out.

She talks again. "But you have to try and help Bob and me. You have to try and show the teachers how smart you are. Otherwise, they won't know."

She pauses. "Miss McGinley called today. She said you paid no attention in class yesterday and didn't understand the story she read to the students. And she told me you ran away from her. Is that true, George?"

I think hard. Is Miss McGinley the woman with her finger pinched in the book?

"Miss McGinley likes you, George. You don't need to be afraid of her, do you?"

"No, I don't need to be afraid of Miss McGinley," I say to Mitzi. She is worried. There is a crease across her brow. I want to stop her worry. It's my fault.

"I'll try not to be afraid of her."

But the crease stays and Mitzi does not smile.

"Can I stop going to the school soon?" I ask.

"No, George. Bob and I want you to keep going to school. We have faith in you. You're very intelligent. You read much better than most fifteen year olds in their own language, and for you English is your *second* language. That *proves* you're intelligent, don't you see?"

"Yes, Mitzi," I answer. "I see. I'll try harder to please Miss . . ."

"McGinley, George." The crease comes to her brow again for a second, then smoothes away. "McGinley."

I say the name and add, "The woman with the book."

"That's right," Mitzi says as she stands. "Bob will be in in a minute to say goodnight. Okay?"

She leans and kisses me on my cheek. Her red hair swishes on the pillow.

I lie and wait for Bob. Soon I hear his feet brush the carpet.

Bob is a big man. His skin is black. But I am not afraid of his skin. He smiles a lot — his whole face is friendly wrinkles then. His black hair is short, like twisted wires.

He sits on the sky blue carpet beside the bed. He is so tall we can talk this way. "How was *Shàolín* class tonight?"

"Good." I answer. "*Shīfu* says I'll be ready for the brown in a month or so."

"Remind me what *Shīfu* means in English, George."

"It means 'Master.'"

"You remember the belts?" This is a game he plays with me.

"I remember, Bob."

"Tell them to me." He leans back on his big hands. Bob has long thin fingers. He plays the piano.

"White — that's, uh, novice — yellow, orange, green, blue — that's me — brown, black first degree, second, and third degree."

"Good man, George," Bob says. A big smile splits his

face. "By the way, Principal up at Elmwood says you dumped your shoes today. That right?"

"I don't know, Bob."

"You know, George. Bare feet. No shoes. You like to go without shoes all the time. We let you do it here, but at old Elmwood they get all uptight when one of the citizens walks around with his toes showin'."

Bob jumps to his feet and yanks the comforter away. He grabs my foot, small in his huge black hand, and tickles it. I begin to shriek.

"Barefoot, buddy," he laughs. "At school. Did you do it?"

I can hardly talk. But I remember now. In the class with the cars. We have to fix the cars. I was at a desk, looking at car pictures in a magazine. I dumped my shoes and socks. A man with a long white coat yelled at me.

"Yes, yes," I say, laughing. "I did it. I won't do it again."

Bob lets go and pulls the sunny comforter up again.

"Good man," he says. "You remembered. We'll get that old memory machine of yours firing on all eight cylinders yet. Meantime, you show your toes around here as much as you want. But at school, well, humor them. Okay? Goodnight, George."

Bob leans way down and I reach up and hug him. His body is hard and strong. His power flows into me.

He leaves the room, turning out the overhead light. He does not shut the door.

Now the shadows own the room. Even though light comes through the door and across the room, near the floor, my night light burns. A yellow pool of safety in the darkness.

馬

I wake up fast, like a dry twig snapping.

I am breathing hard and my muscles are twisted tight. I can feel the sweat trickle. I have had The Dream again.

I try to control my breathing, like Bob showed me. My eyes dart to the wall. The light is still there, glowing across the dark floor. My comforter has slipped to the floor and the sheet is twisted around me, like a thick rope. I breathe in and out, in and out, slowly.

I untangle the sheet and pull the comforter up onto me again. Slowly I force myself to face The Dream. Mitzi and Bob said I have to do this. I have to review The Dream to conquer it.

The jungle is there in the distance, looming, like a black smudge against a dull sky. The terror. I float toward the smudge until I stand at the edge. I stare into the thick gloom. Tangles of wet trees and vines. Water drips. A rasping sound begins, then swells. A voice is screaming over and over, screaming from a black mouth, over broken teeth. There is a path in the jungle, with a hole. The screams come from the hole.

I float again and then I am standing on a sharp rock. Around me a tossing, boiling ocean stretches into the gray sky. Wind whips spray into my face. The wind screams from a black mouth, over broken teeth. Away in the distance a ship rears and plunges. Over the side of the ship something pours into the tossing waves. It is people. They disappear.

I turn and run. I am in a black tunnel. I hear ragged breathing. My feet squelch in the wet clay. Something alive screeches. I run fast but do not move. Something is after me. The ship is chasing me. The voice from the jungle is chasing me. The tunnel disappears and I begin to fall, down and down. A voice screams, "It's you! It's you! It's your fault!"

This is where I wake up.

Reviewing The Dream calms me but it makes me cry.

Sobs tear from deep inside me and toss like waves in my chest. I sit up in bed and pull the comforter around me, bury my head in the folds of the cloth.

I have made something terrible happen, but I don't know what it is.

I will wait like this until I see a crack of light from under the window curtains. I will be able to sleep then.

2

School is eight blocks up the hill from Bob and Mitzi's house and one block to the left. On the way home, it's reversed. When I am on my way out the kitchen door I read the list tacked on the door for me: *Bedroom tidy? Got your books? Got your lunch? Say in your mind how to get to school.* I say it.

The school parking lot is crowded. Morning sun blazes from some of the car windows. The Black Ones are there, leaning against a car, laughing and shouting. Their laughter is sharp and hard. A cigaret passes back and forth. There are six of them, all wearing black leather jackets. Their shadows are bunched together.

As I pass, one shouts, "Hey, Rice!" The others laugh.

I do not know why they call me Rice. My name is George. I keep walking.

"Hey, Rice. You come here when I'm talking to you."

One of them is in front of me, now. He puts his hands

on my shoulders and turns me around and pushes me toward the others.

The leader sits on the hood of the car. He is a big guy, dressed all in black. His hair is long and greasy. His face is spotted with angry red pimples.

I am standing in front of him now, looking up at him. The other Black Ones are behind me, laughing and passing the cigaret around.

The leader jabs the air in front of my face with his finger. "Listen, Rice," he sneers, "I thought I told you not to come across this parking lot any more."

I say nothing. I do not know what to say. I feel danger coming from the Black Ones, like a bad odor.

"Ah, he's just a stupid dummie," says a voice from behind me. "Probably doesn't know what a parking lot *is*!"

Mocking laughter from behind me. Then a voice. "Yeah, he's in the Dummies' Class. Aren't you, Rice?" A fist punches my shoulder. "You got no brain between your ears. Just rice."

The leader jumps down from the hood of the car. He moves awkwardly. He stands so close I can smell his breath. He is much taller than I, and a little fat.

"Hold his arms," he snarls. "It's about time this little door knob learned a lesson." He draws a wide leather belt from his waist and begins to roll it around his fist. "It's about time he learned who runs this school."

I try to side-step away, but they have already got me. My arms are jerked behind my back and up. An arrow of pain shoots across my shoulders. The belt thickens around the fist. There is a big silver buckle on the end.

"Here! What do you think you're doing? Stop that!" A woman's voice cuts the air.

The Black Ones let go of my arms but the leader grabs my shirt front and twists. He is ready to strike. I can see it in his eyes. Without thinking I step back and turn. His grip breaks easily because he has been thrown off by the voice. The red spots on his face flare in anger.

The voice is closer. "Stop that! Leave him alone!"

It is the thin blonde teacher. Her voice is angry but her hands tremble and her eyes dart from one Black One to another.

"Stay out of this," snarls the leader. "Mind your own damn business."

Quickly she grabs my hand and leads me toward the school. Her thin hand is cold and clammy. Behind us a voice calls, "We'll get you for this, lady."

We hurry toward the school. Other kids going our way stare as we pass.

"Stay away from those boys, George," she says in a shaky voice. "They're dangerous. Do they bother you often?"

Her fear begins to seep into me, like a stain. I am afraid now, too. I want to get away from her.

"Sometimes," I answer. I begin to run. I enter the big glass door ahead of her and lose myself among the crowds hurrying through the halls.

I go into the washroom near the office, the one with the big blue sign on the door. There is no one there. I look at the face in the mirror above the big half-circle sink. What is wrong with my face? Why do the Black Ones laugh at me?

As I stare at the face that is lost in the shadows I begin to feel myself slide away into The Well. My hands grip the edge of the sink. My fingernails scrape on the stone.

Behind me, the door bangs open, slamming against the short wall that shields the room. The noise snaps me back. I hear a small electric motor. Wheels appear from behind the wall — big, thin wheels, with narrow rubber tires. The light bounces off the shiny spokes. The motor's sound changes and in comes a wheelchair.

The chair is made of shiny metal tubes with pads on the arms. A boy sits in it. His feet rest on small platforms. Inside his jeans his legs are thin, like the tubes the chair is made of. His body seems broken at the waist, but above his waist his body stretches the red cloth of his shirt. Where his right hand should be a shiny metal hook sticks out of his sleeve. The hook is sort of double, two hooks side by side joined at the base. He has a friendly face, with brown eyes and short, curly black hair.

"How are ya?" he says, smiling. His teeth are strong and even.

I do not answer, but he doesn't seem to mind.

"Took me ages to find this can. Have to do something about that door. Absolutely. What's your name?"

"George."

"Mine's Hook. For obvious reasons," he adds, and smiles again. His smile is warm, like Bob's. It makes me feel safe.

"My real name is Hey-soos," he goes on. "It's spelled J-E-S-U-S. It's a Spanish name. My mother named me after my grandfather. He came here from Spain about a million years ago. Nobody calls me that, though. Too hard to pronounce. And the teachers get all upset when you tell them your name's Jesus. Kids at my old school called me Zeus for short, but that was before I got this."

He holds up the hook. Where it joins his arm there is a band of black leather.

"I'm new here, George. Just enrolled today. Filled in all their forms and here I am. My Uncle Brian is the Guidance Head so I got through the hoops fast. What about you? You new here, too?"

I think hard for a few seconds.

"No. Not new. I started when . . . when school started."

A strange look crosses his face.

"You mean, at the beginning of September? After Labor Day?"

"I . . . guess so."

"But I mean, did you come to this school before that? Last year?"

"I don't know. I don't think so."

I can tell he wants to ask more. He looks confused. But he changes the subject.

"Well. Hey, George, maybe you can show me around the school. What do you say?"

I begin to feel uneasy and move toward the door.

"No. I can't."

His hook pulls back on a tiny metal stick at the end of the chair arm. With a quiet whirr, the chair rolls back and blocks my way.

"What's the matter, George? Did I say something wrong? Are you mad about something?"

I stop and look down at him. At his eyes. I relax a little. Something about him makes me feel he won't pin me down. He won't try to trap me with questions I can't answer. Maybe because he's weak, too.

"No. Nothing you said. I can't show you around the school. I don't know things."

"Oh, so you *are* new here, like me. Well —"

"No. I don't *remember* things!" I almost shout. "I don't remember things."

The motor whirrs again as Hook guides the chair over to the sink. He begins to wash his hands. Or, hand.

"Me, too," he says over his shoulder. "I'd forget my head if it wasn't bolted on." He laughs.

"No, it's *different*, Hook. I can't remember *anything*. That's why I'm in the Special Class."

Whirr of the motor. He reaches up with the hook, pinches a paper towel, and jerks it out of the container on the wall. He takes half a minute to dry his hand.

"Did I ever tell you the nickname they gave me at my old school, George?" The balled up towel loops into the waste container.

"Yeah. Uh, Zooss or something."

Whirr, the chair turns. Hook has on a big, wide smile.

"Hey George."

"What?"

"You remembered."

I can feel my jaw drop and a warm flush swell into my face. I'm mixed up. I turn to leave.

"Catch you later, George," he calls out as the door hisses shut behind me. Inside, I hear the motor start up again.

馬

I feel relief now that I'm leaving the school for home. One block over and eight blocks down the hill. But first I walk down the lane between the rows of trees that lead from the school to Elmwood Avenue. The trees throw long shadows across the ground. I turn right and walk along the edge of the parking lot, inside the chain-link fence. I don't want to cross the middle of the lot. I forget why.

Ahead of me is the gate, where there is a wide driveway onto Elmwood. Cars turn in and out, picking up students. A school bus creeps in like a yellow caterpillar, eats up a crowd of laughing kids, then crawls away again. I can see the bright faces of the kids in the windows.

As the bus moves away, I see the Black Ones in a bunch. Now I remember why I can't cross the lot.

I stop. A pang of disappointment cuts into me, like a thin blade.

Hook is with them.

The Black Ones are in a knot around the wheelchair. I'm too far away to see Hook's face. The chair begins to move away from them toward the fence and they all wave, laughing, watching the chair go. But the laughing has mockery in it. Maybe Hook isn't friends with them after all.

I watch him as the chair moves slowly, straight toward the fence. Where is he going? I wonder. Then the chair lurches and begins to head toward the gate.

Two cars and a bus are jammed up there, waiting for a break in the traffic. Still the wheelchair creeps on its new course. It is near the gate now. The traffic on Elmwood clears and the cars and bus move away. As the chair gets to the gate I can see Hook better.

His face is rigid with terror.

His arms are tied to the chair.

I start to run just as the chair passes through the gate. A car cuts in front of it, barely missing Hook, turning into the lot on squealing tires. A kid sticks her head out the rear window, hair streaming, and shouts, "You're on the wrong race track, hamburger!"

The chair reaches the street just as I dash through the gate. A long red station wagon, packed tight with students, swerves to avoid the chair and roars past. The chair is on the street when I get to it. I can hear Hook making fear noises back in his throat. His face is white.

A car flashes past in the other lane. There is a bus coming straight for us. Blare of the horn. Squeal of brakes. I grab the handles of the chair and heave backwards. It is heavy and the wheels, driven by the motor, churn forward. The bus is close. I can hear the engine growling. I can see dead insects plastered to the flat steel nose. I gather all my strength, yell *"Hài!"* as I heave again and drag the chair up over the curb and onto the grass.

The bus grinds past and the horn blares again. Faces are pushed against the windows, staring. The motor on the chair pops and spits out sparks and a puff of smelly white smoke. The wheels stop churning up the grass just as my hands slip off the handles and I fall back.

"Get me into the school, George," Hook gasps. "Quick. *Please.*"

I scramble to my feet and look down at him. Fear soaks the air around him. There is a heavy acid smell, too, and I notice his jeans are wet at the crotch.

The chair is heavy but moves freely after Hook releases a little lever. I push quickly across the lot, weaving between the parked cars. The Black Ones are gone and most of the buses have pulled out.

I know what Hook wants. I get him through the big double doors and into the washroom with the blue sign.

Once inside, he breathes easier. I untie the thick dirty string that holds his arms to the chair. The color is starting to come back to his face. He swallows hard a couple of times then leans over the sink, awkwardly, and splashes water on his face. I hand him a paper towel.

"God, George," he says, wiping his face. "You saved my life!" He turns the chair and looks at me. "If you hadn't been there I'd be splattered all over the grille of that bus! I was never so scared in my life. Absolutely!"

I say nothing. I don't know what to say.

After a minute he says, "Hey George. Who *are* those guys?"

"The Black Ones."

"That a gang or something?"

"I'm not allowed to cross the parking lot."

He gives me a strange look. "What a sweet bunch! They have a great way of making a new guy feel welcome around here. They almost killed me. Absolutely."

He talks fast, nervous. "They didn't *mean* to hurt me. They aimed me at the fence. Guess they thought I'd look really funny, tied to my chair, wheeling into the chain link, stuck there. They didn't *mean* to hurt me," he repeated. "But one of the wheels hit a rock and I changed direction."

I do not answer. I study his face. I see things there I understand. His no-power feeling as the chair carried him like an egg into the traffic. His burning anger at the jeers of the Black Ones. His smallness feeling.

Maybe the shadows own his legs.

I can see the water gathering in his eyes. His voice is small and weak. "Look at me, dammit! Pissed my pants. Stuck in this pile of nuts and bolts. *Helpless!*"

His body sags. His strength is gone.

He stops. I know this is not a time to talk.

I feel strange. I know he feels bad and I feel bad *with* him, *for* him. But I feel . . . *good*, too. Why? I wonder. Because I helped him?

He talks again. "You know, George, most of the time I can handle it, but every once in a while I *hate* being a cripple. God, I hate it!"

He looks down. A tear plops onto his wet lap.

He sits like that for a few minutes.

Before I know it, the words are out of my mouth. "I'm a cripple, too, Hook."

I don't know why I say it. But I know I am. Like Hook, but different.

He looks up at me, wiping each eye with the back of his left hand. He smiles. Strength seems to flow back into him.

"What a pair we are, eh, George? Absolutely. You with no memory bank, me with no stilts and a fish hook for a hand. We oughta team up. George and the Dragon."

He laughs, his head back. Then he puts out his left hand.

"Shake, George. Friends for life. Okay?"

Awkwardly, I shake hands with him.

"Okay, Hook. Friends for life."

At the front door of the school a blue and white van is parked. On the side, big letters say BARRIE KIWANIS WHEEL TRANSIT. A side door opens and a little elevator drops to the pavement. I roll Hook onto the elevator. The driver pulls a switch and Hook rises to the level of the van's floor. The driver hauls the chair in and locks it in place next to a window.

As the van pulls away, Hook slides the window back and sticks his head out.

"I just got a brilliant idea, George. Absolutely. Catch you later and tell you about it."

I start walking home. One block over and eight blocks down the hill. On the way to school, it's reversed.

3

"Three milk glasses, George."

"Oh yeah. Okay."

I am setting the table for supper and Mitzi is at the stove. Delicious smells rise from two big pots. Warm afternoon sunshine streams in the window and splashes over the kitchen table.

I count the place settings again after putting down the three glasses. The dishes look nice and neat on the red checkered tablecloth.

Mitzi says setting the table is good practice.

A car pulls in the driveway and stops outside the kitchen window. The horn beeps twice as the engine quits. Slam of a door. Bob barges into the kitchen, letting the metal screen door slap shut behind him. He puts his lunch pail down on the sideboard. Then he hangs his windbreaker on a hook by the door and kicks off his work boots.

"Hi Family," says his deep voice.

He kisses Mitzi on his way to the sink. He turns on the taps and begins to lather up his big hands.

"Supper ready?" he asks. "I'm starved. Two rush jobs today. Sometimes I wish that foreman would go away and quit bothering us. He'd get twice the work out of the toolroom if *he'd* get out. How's it goin', George?" he asks, and lobs the towel at my head.

I catch it easily, flip it back, and he hangs it on the rack above the sink.

"Fine, Bob." I pour milk into the three glasses carefully, watching the bubbles foam and churn their way up the sides. Bob and I sit down at the round table. He's on my right, with his back to the window.

Mitzi plunks the big pots on the table, one at a time.

"What's on for tonight?" Bob says. "Elephant ears or goats' feet? I sure hope it's goats' feet, because I know George *hates* —"

"Since it's Friday night," Mitzi cuts in, "and for once you're not working overtime tomorrow, we have . . ." she lifts a pot lid with a mittened hand and a puffball of steam boils out. ". . . beef stroganoff in this pot —"

"All right!" Bob shouts. "Lemme at it."

"And in this pot," another cloud of steam, "we have . . . rice!"

Rice.

A bar of light blinks on in my head.

Rice.

I can feel myself slipping away. Bob's and Mitzi's voices are cut to low volume. But I'm not scared. This is not like slipping into The Well.

The bar of light in my head widens. A glint of bright metal. Big yellow bus with faces pushed against the windows, staring.

I hear the fridge motor click on, then whirr.

"What's that you said, George?" asks Bob. There is worry in his voice.

"Rice," I hear myself murmur from a long way off. "That's what they call me."

"Who? Who calls you that?" Mitzi's voice is tight.

I blink and shake my head. There is a small heap of snowy rice on each of our plates, topped with meat in steaming brown gravy. The sunlight from the window glints on the spikes of the fork in Mitzi's hand. I look over at Bob. His mouth is full of food but he isn't chewing.

They are waiting for something.

"The Black Ones. They call me 'Rice.' I can't cross the parking lot."

The light in my head is growing. I no longer feel that I'm slipping backwards. I'm here, in the kitchen. I hear them breathing. The fridge motor still whirrs.

"Say some more, George," is all Bob says past his mouthful of stroganoff. His eyes are clear, pinning me.

I start to talk. A jumble of things, like . . . like when you look at a bunch of snapshots, one by one. Then I can feel it coming together. I can *feel* it fitting.

I am telling them about the Black Ones. About Hook. The wheelchair rolling into the traffic.

When I finish, I stop like a radio shut off. The fridge motor has stopped. There is no steam coming off our plates.

I look at Mitzi. Her face is blank. I turn to Bob. His chin trembles.

"This is it," he says. His voice is low and shaky. "This is it. I *knew* it would come."

"Take it easy, Bob." Mitzi is talking quietly. "This may be a . . . a sort of fluke. We shouldn't base too much on one time."

I look at her. She is still holding her fork, in the same

position. It trembles a little. She looks at it, then puts it down slowly. She sweeps her hair away from her face and tucks it behind her ears. It makes her look like a little kid.

Her words say we should be careful but her voice says she wants to agree with Bob.

"Let's just go easy," she adds.

Bob is grinning. "Hey, George." He pokes me in the ribs with a thick forefinger. "Where are we going tonight? What do you do on Friday nights?"

It's a test. His eyes are wide and a big grin splits his face. He expects me to pass.

"Uh, I go to *Shàolín* practice. Uh, twice a week, Tuesdays and Fridays."

"Right on, George. What do you think now?" he asks Mitzi.

Before she can answer I tell him, "I cheated, Bob. I figured out it *had* to be *Shàolín* practice. It's the only thing I do at nights. It *had* to be that. It doesn't *mean* anything."

Bob's smile gets wider and he throws his arms out like he wants to hug the two of us at once. He laughs low, back in his throat. But I don't feel so good. For a minute I felt great. But I *had* tricked him about the practices. I didn't remember anything. I just figured out what he was getting at.

"No, George." There is sureness in Mitzi's tone now. "Don't you see? How could you answer Bob if you didn't remember about the practices? You couldn't trick him if you didn't remember that's the only thing you do at nights."

I see she's right. I can feel a smile creeping over my face.

"Okay!" Bob rubs his hands together. He is using his Planning Voice. "Monday morning we go over to the school and talk to the principal and guidance head. We get you out of that so-called Special Class. But in the meantime, tonight, after practice, we hit the Video Van and pick up a bunch of movies. Then the pizza parlor for a 'superdisk.' What movie do you want first, George?"

"*Karate Kid*," I answer right away. "And," I think for a second, "and lots of pepperoni on the pizza." And I start to laugh. I can't stop.

Because things are changing. I can feel them changing.

Bob puts his hands on the table. The long fingers are spread wide. His voice gets serious.

"Listen, George. I'm — we're —" he nods at Mitzi, "we're proud of you. Tonight is a big night. But tonight isn't everything. You'll probably improve slowly."

"And you may have regressions," Mitzi adds.

"Have what?"

"Regressions," she says. "It means you may slide backwards a bit. But you'll improve. That's what the doctor said. He laid it all out and, so far, it's happened very much as he said. He told us, if you ever got your memory back, it would happen like this. Something — nobody knew what — would trigger things. Well, for some reason, what you did for this Hook guy — saving his life, it sounds like — was the trigger. And now, all of a sudden, you can pull a lot of stuff out of your head when you want it."

Bob cuts in. "But he also said things would improve *slowly*. And as your memory gets better, it will be spotty. I mean, your memory will come back in bits and pieces. And the pieces won't always fit together in the right order. So don't be too impatient."

"*You* should talk about impatience!" Mitzi laughs.

Then she begins to reheat the supper. We eat fast so I can get to practice on time and Bob talks as we eat.

But on the way to the gym in the car I am thinking. What about The Well? Will I fall into The Well any more? And will I still have The Dream?

4

Mitzi is nervous as the secretary shows us into the principal's office.

Before we went in she said, "I hate schools, George. Every time I go into one I feel like a student again. And I was in the principal's office *far* too often as a kid."

She has on her good green dress. She wears her hair long.

The principal gets up and comes out from behind his big desk. He is taller than Mitzi. He wears a dark blue suit. The skin at his neck is loose and pinched by his collar. He has a fringe of white hair around his bald spot. His face is friendly.

After we sit down, he and Mitzi talk about the weather. I look out the big windows of the office. It's a gray day and the wind is snatching a few leaves from the trees along the lane down to Elmwood Avenue.

There is a knock on the door and another man comes in

and sits in the chair by the door. He is very tall with a body like a stick and a long, thin face. He smiles and waits.

"I've asked Mr. Bronson to join us, Mrs. Steele. He's the Head of the Guidance Department, and familiar with George's, ah, case. Now, before we begin to discuss the matter of George's, ah, placement in the Special Class, I wonder if it wouldn't be better if George waited for us in the outer office."

Mitzi shakes her head immediately. Her hair swings back and forth across her back.

"No. Bob — Mr. Steele — and I feel that this concerns George, so he should be a part of it."

"I only thought," says the principal, "that this discussion might be a little, ah, delicate and might make George a little uncomfortable."

"That's all right, Mr. Watson. George will be fine." And she turns and smiles to me. "Right, George?"

I am sitting behind her and to the right on a couch against the wall. I nod.

The principal asks Mitzi to tell him why she thinks I should be "placed in the regular program." As she talks, explaining what happened last Friday in our kitchen, the principal flips through a file in front of him. He nods a lot. Every minute or so he says, "Uh huh," or "Yes, I see."

Mitzi is talking fast because she's nervous. That makes me nervous. I begin to get the trapped feeling. I begin to wish I could go. I want to leave, to slip into the washroom next door and take it easy.

Then I look over at Mr. Bronson. He looks at ease. With long fingers he fiddles with a button on his sweater.

He winks at me.

I don't know what it means, but I begin to relax a little.

"I understand your concerns," the principal is saying, "and I sympathize. We all want what's best for George, of course. But I wonder if you've thought about the effect of this change on George."

Somewhere a bell rings faintly and a stream of guys dressed in blue gym shorts and orange Elmwood T-shirts flows from a doorway onto the football field. They must be cold. The teacher, dressed in long pants and a track top, follows. He is walking.

Mitzi is answering. "Of course we have. That's why we're here. We think the class he is in now is for slow learners. George isn't a slow learner. He's very intelligent, and now that he's made this, sort of, breakthrough, or whatever you want to call it, he should be able to handle regular classes. Why? What's the problem here?"

The principal sits back in his chair.

"Well, we *hope* there won't be a problem. But, frankly Mrs. Steele, we — Mr. Bronson and I — think the change would be too abrupt. At present, George takes all his academic classes with Miss McGinley, plus one shop — auto — with Mr. Pendleton. That's one class change a day, with work at what is obviously a simple and undemanding level. The regular program requires three class changes a day, four new teachers, and a *very heavy* demand on George's memory."

He pauses and leans forward to close the file.

"Our concern here is not *whether* George should change programs — he should — but when and how."

"So you think we're moving too fast on this?" Mitzi asks.

The kids outside are tossing footballs around. The teacher is shouting and blowing his whistle a lot.

The principal's voice is calm. "We think so, yes."

I can see Mitzi's shoulders sag a little. She turns and looks at me. The crease is across her brow. She turns back.

"But we *think* we may have a compromise, Mrs. Steele. A rather, ah, unusual solution. It would require your permission, of course. Mr. Bronson will explain."

As Mr. Bronson talks, his hands are never still. They fly up like birds to his chin, his tie, a sweater button, then fall back to rest on the chair arms. But only for a second. He mentions Hook, but uses his real name. He pronounces it *Hey-soos* like Hook does. He says he's Hook's uncle. He knows about the almost accident.

He asks if Mitzi will agree to let me help Hook. "George could help Jesus, who now refuses to use the motorized chair. He has a bit of trouble, as you may imagine, pushing a regular chair himself. This way, George will benefit, too. He will be attending regular classes, but without the *pressure*, if you see what I mean. Jesus will help George remember things. We'll leave George officially enrolled where he is, so he can get his credits based on the easier program, and when you — and he, of course —think he's ready, we'll simply tell the computer to switch George to the regular program officially."

He smiles, then winks at me again.

Mitzi is silent for a few seconds. The principal shifts his weight and his chair squeaks. A bell rings again and the orange T-shirts stream back into the school. The teacher follows slowly.

"Well," Mitzi says finally, "I don't know what to think. This is quite a surprise."

"We think it will work, Mrs. Steele," the principal answers.

"What does the other boy . . ."

"Jesus," puts in Mr. Bronson. His hand flutters to his thinning hair.

"Yes . . . would he agree?"

"Let's ask him," Mr. Bronson says. He gets up fast and leaves the office. Hook must have been waiting outside because he rolls in, pushed by Mr. Bronson. He has on one of the orange T-shirts. He greets the adults politely. He is not nervous.

"Hi, George. How's it goin'?"

He looks over to his uncle, who has sat down again. Mr. Bronson nods.

"What do you say, George? I could use a little help. If I push this vehicle with one hand I just spin around in circles." He laughs. "It's a team job. St. George and the Dragon. How about it?"

The two men look at me. Mitzi looks at me.

Before she can ask, I say, "Yeah. I want to."

5

"George! George!"

The voice is low and far away. It gets louder, like when a radio is turned up slowly.

I need to run, to escape. Or hide inside or under something. The need is bigger than my terror. I try to run but something is holding me tightly around my chest. I struggle, thrashing my arms and legs in the dark. I can't escape.

I can hear another voice, tearing my brain, like thin paper ripped again and again. "Tell me! Tell me! Tell me!" it screams.

It is my voice.

I stop. My ears fill with the sound of my wild breathing.

"George. It's all right. We're here."

That is Mitzi's voice. It soaks the fear away and my rigid body relaxes. I open my eyes. She is holding me and Bob is standing beside the bed. The room is filled with yellow light. My breathing slows. I can feel sweat trickle under my pajamas.

"Okay, now, take it easy." Mitzi's voice comes from behind my head. She still grips me in a bear hug.

Bob sits down on the carpet beside the bed. "It's The Dream again, right, George?" He tries to sound natural, as if he's asking about school or *Shàolin* practice. He smiles a thin smile.

"Yes," I hear myself say. My head throbs. The pain pushes at the back of my eyes. "This time was the worst yet."

Mitzi lets go. "Review The Dream, George," she says as she gets to her feet. "I'll get you some hot chocolate."

The Dream was the same but different. The jungle was there, black with terror. Floating like a black lake in the gray sky. And the screams, from a black mouth, over broken teeth.

Then there were dead people, grownups and kids, lying in ditches. I did not know them. Next, I stood on the rock again, surrounded by wild wind and tossing waves. Hands reached from the waves for my legs. They clutched my ankles. Faces, white and puffed like mushrooms, came to the surface and disappeared. I *knew* them, the way you know things in dreams, but I did not recognize them. I jumped into the crashing waves but found myself in the tunnel, running. Running away. And the hollow voices shouted, "It's you! It's you! It's your fault!"

I tell Bob The Dream. He sits quietly, leaning back on his arms. His big hands are spread wide on the blue carpet.

"This is the first time you've sort of, well, talked back to the voice in your dream," he comments. "The voice is blaming you for something, right? But it doesn't say what. And now you're asking. You're saying, 'Tell me what's my fault.'"

I don't say anything. The fear is going away slowly, but I am still a little numb. I sit up straight and swing my legs over the edge of the bed.

Mitzi comes back with three mugs of steaming chocolate on a tray and hands them around. She pulls the chair away from the desk and sits down.

She has heard what Bob said, and continues. "Try to understand this, George. The voice in The Dream is yours, too. You're blaming *yourself* for something — we don't know what — and you're asking yourself what you did wrong. Whatever that thing is, it's locked up in your memory. Do you understand me so far?"

"Yeah, I think so." The wound-up-tight muscles at the back of my neck are beginning to loosen, and the pain in my head is losing some sharpness. I sip the strong, sweet chocolate. Small sips, because it's very hot.

"Now, I want to tell you *why* you don't remember. Something happened to you, something really bad and scary. Sometimes a part of your mind will actually push a bad memory aside — bury it — so the rest of your mind, the conscious, awake part, doesn't have to face it. In a way, your mind is protecting itself. It's protecting itself from the pain the bad memory will cause. Okay?"

She lifts the mug from the desk and takes a swallow. She holds the mug by the handle, her other hand cupping the bottom.

She talks again. "We — Bob, the doctor, and I — think that whatever this thing that happened to you is, it's what messed up your memory. You've been improving fast over the last month, since you met Hook, and this change in The Dream is probably a good sign. Slowly that scary memory is coming to the surface."

Bob shifts his position. He is cross-legged now, and leans his long arms on his knees. "Here's the situation, George," he says. His voice is strong but quiet. "It's going to be tough on you if — when — this bad memory comes into the light. It'll be painful. But I want you to remember two things."

He holds up one finger. The underside is almost pink. "One. Bad memories are never really as bad as they seem. I don't know how to explain this well. As long as the memory stays hidden, it seems really awful. But once it comes into the light, you'll find that you can handle it. You *can*. Got it?"

"Got it," I say, but I don't feel as sure as Bob sounds.

"Two," he goes on. "When things get rough, think of the people who love you. Mitzi, and me, and your friend, Hook. That's important, George. Knowing that people care about you helps a lot."

The three of us sit quietly for a minute or so, drinking. Mitzi asks Bob and me if we want more chocolate. We say no.

"Bob? Mitzi? Who am I? Where did I come from? I mean, I'm not from Canada, am I?"

Bob surprises me. I am serious, but he smiles. He gives out a low, short laugh and looks over at Mitzi.

She notices my reaction. "Bob isn't laughing at you, George."

"No, 'course not." His face looks serious again. "I'm pleased with you. You know, you've *never* asked us that before! Really, you haven't. This is great!" Bob leans back on his hands again.

"Okay, here goes," he begins. I climb into the bed and pull the covers to my waist, leaning back on the headboard.

"You've always known that we're not your real parents. Well, we got you almost two years ago through the United Church organization that tries to find homes for kids. Some are orphans. Some are refugees."

"What's a —"

"Wait. I'll explain. This organization won't always tell foster parents all about a kid's background. It depends on the situation. Sometimes they don't know themselves. Anyway, all we know about you is that you were brought to Canada from Hong Kong."

Bob springs up and snatches the world globe off my desk. The bed sinks down as he sits. He points to a pink part and says, "This is Canada. And here, by my finger-nail, is where we live. Now, follow my finger."

He traces a line across the pink, turning the globe as his finger moves across the blue part and then down to a dot.

"This city is Hong Kong. The United Church has an agency there, too, a big one. They're the people who sent you to Canada. That's all we know for sure. Like I said, you may be an orphan, or a refugee. That's a person who has to run away from the country he was born in, sometimes because there's a war, sometimes because there's government problems."

Bob slides his finger back and forth across a big part of the globe. "If you *are* a refugee, George, you could be from one of these countries around here."

"Name some, Bob."

"Well, there's Kampuchea, Vietnam, China, Korea. Or maybe your parents lived in Thailand — here. Who knows? It's all very, very complicated sometimes."

The names sound mysterious to me. They have no meaning. But I can see they are real places. I can read the words on the globe and see the twisting blue lines where one country leaves off and another begins.

"How do you know it's one of *those* places?"

"Well, because you're Asian, George."

"What's that?"

"Let's look. Come on, Mitzi."

Bob draws us across the room to stand in front of my dresser. Our faces appear in the mirror. I'm in the middle.

Mitzi has pale skin, with a few freckles, and long, very red hair. Bob's face is black. His nose is wide and flat and he has a wide mouth.

The face in the middle is mine. I stare. The dark eyes, the dark hair.

My skin color is hard to name. It's not black or pale. It's not *between* Mitzi and Bob. It's almost light yellow, but not. I'm like *Shifu*.

I begin to tremble.

Because it hits me suddenly. I am seeing *all* of my face. *All* of it is in the light. It's who I am. The shadows are gone.

Bob's face moves behind me. Now it's above mine, wearing a wide grin. I feel his hands on my shoulders.

"Now, *that*," he says, "is one hell of a handsome Asian face."

I am back in my bed and the lights are out. My door is open and the night light near the floor glows. Names of countries spin through my head, like the globe spins on its shaft. And before my eyes I see the three faces.

I know what I have to do now. I know I have help.

I get out of bed and open the curtains. The window is a black rectangle. I get back into bed and pull the covers up. I am not afraid. Tonight the fear is gone.

6

It's a really nice October day so Hook and I decide to eat lunch outside. We go — me pushing, Hook talking — looking for some dry ground under one of the trees in the lane in front of the school. We find a good spot.

Hook announces, "This will do, absolutely," and locks the wheels of the chair. Then he begins struggling.

"What are you doing?" I ask.

"Getting out. I wanna sit on the ground and lean up against that tree. No fun having a picnic in this steel seat."

I move to help him out. I can't figure how he'll do it on his own.

But he pushes my arms away. "*I can do it!*" he almost shouts.

I step back, surprised. His body goes limp and he settles back in the chair.

"Sorry, George. You didn't deserve that. It's just that I want to do this by myself."

"That's okay. Forget it."

"I will if you won't."

He laughs at his joke and begins again. He creeps his body forward on the seat, using his forearms as levers on the chair arms. He stops and grasps each leg by the pant cloth at the knee, then lifts it, clearing the foot off the pedal.

"I worked this out all by myself. It's not perfect yet, but it'll do. When I get it all set, I'll patent the process and make a million bucks."

I do not know what patent means, but I don't ask. I am watching as he flips the platforms out of the way and places his legs together, slanting to his left from the knee. He begins to creep forward again to the edge of the seat. His left hand grips the end of the armrest and he leans his weight onto his right arm. The bright hook projects.

There is not very much effort. I can see that. His upper body is strong. The problem is balance.

He begins to lower himself. His legs fold under him like strips of cloth. But just as it looks like he'll make it, with his behind almost to the ground, the chair slips backward, locked wheels skidding on the grass. Hook loses his balance and flops to the side, grunting.

As he pushes himself upright again and begins to lever his body to the big tree, he says, "Still haven't got it down pat, see? But it's coming."

The tree still has enough leaves to give us some shade. The brown grass is dry and the ground is not cold. This is a big tree, with shaggy bark. We can't see each other. Hook is propped so that he looks across the football field and track to the gym wing of the school. I'm facing Elmwood. I can see the gate where Hook almost got hit by the bus.

I take off my shoes and socks, wiggling my toes. It feels good.

We eat in silence for a while. I got peanut butter, as

usual, and an apple. I can hear Hook crunching, so I guess he got vegetables.

"You know, George," he says, munching, "I'm surprised there aren't more of us at this school by now."

"More of us?"

"Yeah, cripples."

It sounds strange, but I don't mind being called a cripple. I like it. Hook and I are different, but this is a big thing we have in common. We belong to — I don't know to what, but that is a feeling I have.

He is talking again. "Ever since the new law, schools have been falling all over themselves getting ready to accept people like us."

"What law, Hook?" I roll up a sandwich wrapper and put it in the bag, then start in on another sandwich. More peanut butter. I can hear him popping open a Coke.

"Want a sip?"

As I hand back the warm Coke he answers. "The new education law. Our province makes a lot of noise about each kid having an equal right to an education at his own level of ability. Like the kids in the Special Class you were in, see? They have a lot of trouble learning stuff, but the schools can't flunk them out like they used to when our parents were kids. They have to keep teaching those kids as much as they can handle. Want some more?"

"No, thanks."

There are a few kids in the parking lot now. I can hear music from the open doors of some cars. The sun is making me sleepy. Hook's voice mixes with the breeze.

"Another group of kids who usually didn't get much chance in regular schools was the handicapped kids. But the law changed that. 'Bout time, too. Now the schools *have* to take us as equals. We belong just as much as the kids who can climb stairs and remember the times tables, and throw a football. Absolutely. So in this area, all the crippled kids go to this school. It's the newest. You've noticed the ramps, right?"

"Yeah. At the outside doors, and . . . and there's one going up to the gym hall."

"Hey, nice memory. That's right. And the elevator to the second floor. Only cripples get keys. They even have that washroom for us. That's where we first met."

"Right." He's talking about the washroom beside the office. The one with a big blue plastic logo of a wheelchair on it. Hook calls it the Cripples' Can.

"Anyway, like I was saying, there's going to be more of us here. My uncle says we're getting about half a dozen. A blind kid. A couple of deaf-mute kids. Some others."

We sit for a while, saying nothing. A couple of senior students are tossing a football around out on the field, yelling orders to each other. We can hear the slap as the ball is caught each time. Farther down the row of trees some girls are smoking, talking quietly, writing in notebooks.

Hook moves his body farther away from the tree and lies stretched out on his back. His head rests on his hand, the hook on his flat stomach. I can see his face now. It has a look I'm beginning to get used to. His eyebrows frown a little and he presses his lips together. It means he's just thought of a good idea.

"You know what we ought to do, George?" His eyes are closed and the breeze flips his hair a little.

I don't answer. He'll answer for me.

"We oughta form a group — all us cripples — so we can help each other out a bit, you know? I mean, all of us are missing *something*, right? With me, legs and a hand. With you, it's memory. Plus this dream you told me about. And not knowing who you are or where you came from. But we're not all missing the *same* things, probably."

Hook is getting excited, like he usually does when he's working on an idea. His eyes open and flip over to me.

"So we can fill in, you know? Sort of *complete* each other. Absolutely."

He sits up, leaning on his arm, and looks at me. "I think we oughta expand the Cripples' Club, George. After all, what's a club with two members? We should bring in those new kids that are coming into the school. What do you think?"

I'm not sure what to say. I don't like meeting people. Strangers scare me. Maybe they'll try to trap me. Or say things I don't understand.

But then I remember how my memory started to come back. It was helping Hook that did it. And feeling that what I did *mattered*. And Hook always asking me stuff, helping me to keep things in my mind.

I have to force myself to say it. "Yeah, Hook. I think we should."

"Okay. Tomorrow I'll talk to my uncle. Maybe he can help us get in touch with some of these kids. This'll be great, George. Absolutely. Toss me another Coke, will you?"

I lean around the tree and fish another Coke from his lunch bag. I toss it to him. He catches it, then pops the zip tab with the hook. Warm brown suds spray over the grass. He lies down again.

The footballers are gone. Now a half dozen girls are booting a soccer ball around. The parking lot gets busier. A black van swerves in the gate and tears down the lot, screeching to a halt. The back doors fly open and some Black Ones tumble out, pushing and shoving each other. I can hear them cursing and laughing. The driver's door opens and the leader swings neatly onto the pavement, slamming the door as he comes around back.

His eyes catch mine and lock in. He stops, says

something to the others that I can't catch. He heads this way. I snap my head around to look at Hook. He looks as if he's sleeping. His eyes are closed and the Coke is balanced on his chest. Should I say something? Maybe the leader isn't coming over here at all. Maybe it just looks like he is.

I can see him out of the corner of my eye, though, and hear his bootheels on the pavement. I can feel myself begin to tremble and I fight to calm myself. *Shifu* says this is important when you feel danger.

His boots leave the pavement and swish through the short grass.

Now he's here. But he's standing over Hook. Close. He hawks up a big gob of phlegm and spits it out into the grass beside Hook's face. He stands, hands in his pockets, looking down. Hook's eyes open, then close again, slowly.

"Did you see that, George?" Hook's voice is low and calm. His eyes are still shut. He smiles and says, "Must have been birdshit."

He lifts his head and takes a long drag on the Coke, keeping his eyes shut, then rebalances it on his chest. "You know where birdshit comes from, don't you, George? A bird's asshole."

The leader's face reddens. His pimples seem to flare. He raises his leg slowly and kicks the can away with the pointed toe of a cowboy boot. The boot is soft leather — I can tell that — and glows from buffing. The heel, toe, and top edge are decorated with silver strips. Silver studs hold the pull tabs on.

The boots are the only clean thing about him. His jeans are rumpled and dirty. His black leather jacket is smeared with oil. Dandruff is sprinkled on the collar and shoulders. His hair is long and greasy.

After the Coke can goes spinning into the grass he stabs

Hook in the side with the same toe. Hook grunts with the pain and tries to sit up. But the leader takes half a step forward and jabs a boot heel into Hook's chest, dead center. He still has his hands in his pockets.

I can hear the air rush out of Hook's lungs. He's halfway up on his elbows but can't get any higher.

"Stay where you are, half-man," growls the leader, "or the next shot goes into that big mouth of yours."

Hook stays put. He says nothing. The silver decorated heel comes off his chest.

"I hear you and the chink here were in yapping to the principal," he says to Hook. I don't know who he means until he looks over at me.

"Right, Rice?" he sneers.

I say nothing. Why does he call me that? That's not my name.

"What's it to you? You writing a book?" Hook smiles.

"Just this. If you jerks tell a story about a certain wheelchair accident, you'll get your faces rearranged. Your face is all you got left, half-man, so you better take care of it. And if the chink gets hit on the head he'll lose the rest of his brain. Which isn't much."

He steps back. There is an evil smile on his face. He kicks Hook again in the soft part of his side, above the hip. Hook yelps and jerks himself upright.

The black boot is too fast. It lashes out twice more, quick as a snake, and Hook grunts. His teeth are clenched. He doesn't want to show the pain, but it ripples across his face.

I find myself on my feet, moving fast. I catch Hook from behind, under the arms, and drag him backwards. Then I step between him and the leader.

The leader grins. "Quick little chink, aren't you? Ready for your turn?"

He is a bad fighter. His moves show on his face before

his body acts. He reaches for my shirt and I sweep his hand away. His smile drops away like a dead leaf and the anger flares again.

I am not afraid. Now that action has started. I can see the head shot coming and use an overhead block. His left hand is knocked up and away. I do not counterattack. I just wait for the next move. It comes clumsily, a right to my stomach. Gliding back half a step I use an open hand block to knock his punch aside. He loses balance a bit as his body follows the arm but he regains it quickly.

A roar of laughter swells in the parking lot and an engine blasts to life. The leader looks over to where his friends are. Another mistake. But I don't take advantage of it.

Someone must be fooling with his van. He is divided. He wants to end this.

"We'll finish this later," he says, and begins to run. The boot heels pound on the pavement.

Hook is levering himself over to the tree behind me.

"Come on, George. Sit down and take it easy. Don't let Silverheels spoil your day."

I relax and do as he says. There is the slam of doors over in the lot and the van takes off, engine roaring.

We sit quiet for a while.

"George, sometime when you're ready, how about telling me where you learned to fight like that?"

"Okay, Hook. Sometime I will."

But I'm thinking. "Hook," I say, half to him, half to myself, "how come you're so strong?"

"Strong? Oh, lifting weights, I guess. I still do it. Mom and I rigged up a —"

"No, I don't mean that. I mean, you seem *sure* of yourself. You're crippled but you still seem *strong*."

He doesn't answer right away. He just looks up through the dead leaves into the blue sky for a minute.

"It's a promise I made to myself," he says slowly. His face goes hard. "It's hard to keep sometimes, too."

I know what he means. That first day in the can, when his weak feeling showed through for a few minutes.

"What was the promise?"

"It'll take awhile to answer that, George." He looks at me, then at his watch. "Half an hour left 'til lunch is over. I guess we've got time."

7

"I never told you how all this happened," Hook says. He holds up the hook, which glints in the sun. "Wasn't all that long ago — early last year. I was on a holiday with my parents and my cousin Jim in Myrtle Beach. That's in the States," he adds when he sees I don't know it.

"Anyway, after a week my cousin and I were pretty bored. The weather was okay, but we didn't have much to do. So I talked him into renting a motorcycle. He took off downtown and came back in an hour with a new Kawasaki.

"I don't think I ever told you this, George, but I've always been a motorcycle nut. I'd driven for a couple of years off-road. That means you ride a special kind of bike, with knobby tires and heavy springs with lots of travel to them, out in the woods or fields, and nobody cares how old you are or whether you have a license or not.

"So, naturally I had to take a whack at the Kawie. I got

on and tore off down a country road near our motel. It was a sunny morning, not too hot yet, and soon as I got rolling I began to feel that *great* feeling I get when I'm on a bike. It's a kind of freedom. The wind slips past, the motor throbs down there between your calves, you can weave and swerve and watch the scenery flash past.

"Well, I was ripping along about fifty-five miles an hour down this two-lane road with fields on each side. Hardly any traffic. What there *was*, though, was one of those big ugly yellow road graders — the ones that look like a praying mantis — coming towards me on the opposite shoulder. He had the blade down, and a little wave of gravel rolled along in front of it. Also, there were two cars coming at me from the same direction as the grader. The first was a big boat of a station wagon. The second I couldn't name at first 'cause all I could see was the roof. He was tailgating the wagon really close.

"Just as the wagon passed the grader, the Camaro — that's what it was — pulled out to pass. It was black, jacked up in the rear end, and loud. His timing was really bad. When he flashed out into my lane he was about fifty yards away from me. I could see the hood rings and pins, a custom grille, and sunlight burning in the square head-lamps. I could also see the driver's eyeballs bug out when he caught sight of me.

"He hit the binders and his tires screeched for a second before he could cut back in behind the wagon. But it was too late. I had already hit the brakes hard, too. I wasn't used to the cycle, so the brakes locked up. When you do that, you've pretty well had it. I lost it. The back wheel came out from under me and I went down, trying to hang onto the bike, to slide along with it. Because if you and the bike separate, it will probably end up bouncing over you a few times before you stop.

"I went across the road right under the grader. They

said I hit the edge of the blade in the small of my back. That's what cancelled the legs. And one of those monster tires rolled over my hand."

Hook is talking very calmly, in a low voice. But there's sweat on his forehead, and he's clearing his throat a lot.

"Anyway, a few months later I was back at home. Got a new wheelchair. Got a new hook on. My road burns and scratches and cuts were pretty well healed up. Also, I had the worst case of feeling sorry for myself the world has ever seen.

"Because, you know, up until then, I had plans. Big plans. I was going to be a big hockey star. Absolutely. Play in the NHL. Get interviewed on *Hockey Night in Canada*. 'Hey, Jesus, like, what do you think of the game so far, eh?' Make a million.

"Because there was — is — only one thing I like better than cycles, and that's hockey. I'm not just bragging, George. They had me scouted when I was twelve. All set to groom me. Hottest center to come out of this area in twenty-five years — that's exactly what they told my parents. I was really riding high."

Hook is really going, now. He forgets to stop and explain things to me — things he knows I don't know about or won't remember.

The soccer ball rolls off the field, right over his legs, but he doesn't seem to notice. A girl runs past to get it, laughing and shouting to her friends out on the field. She kicks it back to them and returns to the game. Behind us a car roars through the lot, squealing its tires.

"All of a sudden," Hook continues, his voice still low, "it's all gone. I can't eat properly — left-handed — and I drop food in my lap all the time. But I can't *feel* the peas or porridge or stew splat onto me. So after every meal I discover a nice little road map of garbage on my pants when I get up from — I mean when I leave the table. I can't get into bed, can't get out of bed, can't leave the house, can't even take a goddam *crap* without Mom hauling me around like an overgrown Barbie doll.

"And I didn't want to learn, either. I didn't *give* a damn. Just watched TV. Let my Mom push, pull, lift, dress, undress, and clean me. I was dead inside. Absolutely.

"Then, after a month or so of no progress, my mom had enough. She was helping me off the can one day, but I wasn't helping *her*. I went into my I-don't-care-if-I-live-or-die-the-world-has-screwed-me tantrum. Shouting and crying in our little bathroom. She got really mad, George. Burning mad. She hauled me into my chair, barrelled into the kitchen, checked the newspaper — why, I didn't know — bundled me and the chair into the car, and tore out of the driveway like a crazy woman."

Hook stops talking and takes a deep breath. Then he starts up again, slower.

"My mother is the quietest person you'd ever want to meet. She's dark, like me, short, and pretty strong. But gentle. Not that day, though.

"We went charging down to Toronto, breaking the speed limit all the way. Mom was acting so strange, I just kept my mouth shut. She parked on a side street just off Bloor, right under a NO PARKING sign — another thing Mom would never do when she was normal. Usually when we went shopping or something she'd spend the whole time worrying that the parking meter would run out.

"Before I knew it we were rolling towards Bloor Street. On the drive to the city I had been glooming away to myself that I'd never be able to drive a car, only half wondering what Mom was up to. Now I was curious. Bloor was lined with people, three deep, all laughing and chattering. Every minute or so they'd clap their hands as if they were watching a show.

"Mom rolled me up behind the rank of people and said in a loud voice, 'Make way, please!' — another thing she had never done in my life. The people parted good-naturedly and I got a front row seat.

"Bloor Street looked strange. No cars. I mean, like, absolutely. What there was though was a thin stream of runners, not moving too fast, men mostly, but a few women. They were all wearing shorts and tank tops 'cause it was a warm, sunny day. Each runner had a big white square pinned to his chest with a number and 'Labatt's International Marathon' printed on it.

"'We missed the first ones,' my mother said from behind me, 'but I think we're in time.'

"I didn't pay much attention because I was looking at an old guy chugging along. He was barely moving. His feet hardly cleared the ground, but he kept working at it, sweaty and pale. And just behind him one young woman was running along with her arm on the shoulder of the guy ahead of her. I realized that she was blind — you know, you could tell by the way she sort of stared off into nothing.

"I looked up the street and saw a sign. It said 20 MILES. No wonder those runners looked like they were towing invisible trailers! A marathon is twenty-six miles and a bit, George. Forty-two kliks. I used to run to get in shape for hockey, but my longest runs were five miles. After five, I was *beat*. This old guy had run *four times* that and he *still* had over six miles to go.

"Down the road, in the direction the runners were coming from, a noise swelled out of the crowd, like a low moan. The road dipped away out of sight almost a hundred yards away, so I couldn't see what everybody was so excited about. Then the moan became louder. I could hear applause and cheering.

"And then I saw them. Wheelchairs. Out in the road, a

half dozen of them. My mom's strange behavior made sense now. The chairs weren't like mine. They were low, streamlined jobs with big thick rings on the rear wheels so the riders could grip them and drive them forward. The cripples looked weird because their bodies pumped up and down, bending forward until their chests hit their useless legs, and on the way down they drove hard on the wheels. Then their bodies rose straight, they took another grip, and snapped their bodies down. They were fairly close together, making good speed now that they were over the hill. They looked like pistons driving up and down inside an engine.

"The crowd around us was clapping, laughing, cheering. I looked up at their faces. I saw admiration there, George. They sure as hell didn't know what it was like, and never would, but they thought those wheelchair guys were heroes. You could *feel* the emotion."

Hook scratches behind his ear with his hook.

"And that wasn't the end of it. Down the road the crowd noise changed again, got louder and more — I don't know — more charged up. I watched the edge of the hill wondering, What next?

"All I saw at first was the top of a guy's head, bobbing up and down in a strange way. Then his face appeared. He had a brush cut and he held his head a little to the side. His upper body came into view and his tank top was plastered to his body. I could see the strain twisting his face. He was really hurting.

"The crowd was roaring by now, cheering, clapping, louder than ever. I saw then why the guy ran with that funny, hopping gait and why his head bobbed. Where his left leg should have been, from the middle of his thigh down, was a mechanical leg made of two metal tubes, hinged at the knee.

"As he ran, he would plant the tube-leg and sort of pivot

forward and a little to the side, then step onto the real leg and hop once before planting the tube-leg again."

Hook moves his arms, stiff, like sticks, to show me what he means.

"And his arms jerked straight up and down instead of driving forward and back like a normal runner's do. Hitch, step-and-hop, hitch, step-and-hop. And he'd been at it for twenty miles.

"I started feeling real bad then, George. Ashamed. *Really* ashamed. The people around me were going wild. 'Go! Go!' they shouted. 'Attaboy!' 'Good man!' — stuff like that. The man beside me was crying. 'Jee-sus!' he kept saying, almost to himself. 'Jesus! *Look* at that guy!' But I just sat there feeling like the worst kind of spoiled little baby in the world. This was what my mom brought me to see. I knew that then.

"Then something really, absolutely strange happened. I looked at his plastic foot. He had a running shoe on it. He had to, or it would get wrecked. But he was also wearing a *sock* on it! A sock, George. A totally, absolutely unnecessary sock. A white one, with blue trim. It was as if he was saying to the world, 'Yeah, well. You wear two socks and so do I. Why the hell not?' It wasn't as if he was hiding the foot. How could he, with that spidery metal leg sticking out of his shorts like some kind of science fiction wonder machine? I mean, the foot looked more real than the leg. No, it was like he was somehow making things *normal*, not in a phony, pretend way, but like he was saying, 'Okay, life is tough. End of philosophy lesson. Now, let's get to work. I got a race to run here. And racers wear socks.'

"That's when I started to cry. There was a strange, boiling mixture of feelings inside my head. I was so ashamed of myself. The way I treated my mom and everybody else who got near enough to get splashed by the poison. Of giving up so easily.

"And at the same time I admired that guy. Watching him lifted me up. I wanted to roll the chair out and go along beside him and talk to him, be his friend, you know?

"But soon he was gone, hopping and jerking along towards the finish line. He finished the race, too. I read about it next day in the paper.

"On the way back home in the car — my mother was driving at her normal, careful speed — I asked her, 'Who is that guy, Mom?'

"She said, without taking her eyes off the road, 'I don't know, Jesus. But if you want, he's *you*.'

"So that's when I made the promise to myself, George. I would never give up. I would try to live my life like he ran that race. I would live my life with a sock on."

Hook looked me in the eye and laughed.

"A white one, with blue trim. Ab-so-lutely!"

8

Hook and I are the first ones to get to Math class today. I park his chair at the back by the window and lock the wheels. Long, empty rows of desks stretch to the front of the big classroom. Outside it is sunny but it was cold walking to school this morning.

Slowly, students begin to filter into the room. They laugh and call out to each other. They are colorfully dressed and happy. They sit down, talk to kids near them, get up again. They toss books and pens to each other. The room fills up with noise as the long rows of desks fill up with students.

I am nervous here. All the kids are smarter than I am. There is no worry on their bright faces. They are never afraid.

A grownup walks in quickly. Tall, with long black hair and wire glasses. He dumps an armload of books and papers on the metal desk at the front, then straightens his tie and buttons his jacket. He looks around at the faces that I can't see, smiles, and claps his hands together twice.

"Okay, let's get at it!" he shouts. Then, when the babble of voices dies, "The mystery of numbers awaits us!"

"Mystery is right," mumbles Hook. He is leaning over his notebook, writing down numbers. He holds his pen awkwardly in his left hand. "Absolutely."

"Harold, get the door, please," the teacher goes on. A fat guy at the back lurches from his desk and shuts the door.

"Hey, Jackie," the teacher says, "how about joining the real world."

The kids laugh and look at a girl in the third row near the front. She sits with her arm slung over the back of her seat, snapping her fingers and bobbing her head. She is wearing black earphones and thin wires dangle to a little black box clipped to her belt. Finally she notices kids staring at her. One hand darts to the black box and the other snatches the phones from her head.

The teacher smiles and runs his hand through his hair. "What are you listening to? Beethoven maybe?"

The kids laugh again. The girl tosses her head and her long brown hair swishes across her back. "Yeah, sure, right. I listen to Old Ludvig every chance I get, sir."

I can't see her face, but she must be smiling. There is laughter in her voice. She is wearing a jean jacket with badges all over the back. A big white one in the shape of a skull says, STEEL FANGS — IN CONCERT.

A boy beside her adds, "Yeah, sir, Jackie's really into Classical." The others laugh again.

"As if I am!" says Jackie and she reaches across the aisle and punches him lightly on the shoulder. "Metal rules; all else are fools."

"I have some Mozart tapes I could lend you, Jackie," the teacher adds. *The Magic Flute* maybe? Interested?"

"No thanks, sir. I think I'll pass."

"Okay. Well, I tried." He sits down, flips open a black binder, and says, "Let's do the attendance and then take up the homework."

The students start opening books in a buzz of conversation as he calls out names. Before he finishes there's a knock on the door.

"Get that, will you, Harold?" the teacher asks.

The short fat guy heaves himself out of the chair again and opens the door. He sits down without looking to see who's there. The principal walks in, followed by a woman and two kids.

"Mr. Kesak, here are your new students," he says, wiping his hand across his bald head. The loose skin above his collar shakes a little when he talks. "And this is Mrs. Jackson. I'll leave them with you. All right?"

"Fine, Mr. Watson. Thank you." He gets out of his chair and whispers something to the kids sitting at the front. Three of them get up and move to empty seats down the rows.

The woman is short and plump. She has on a black dress and white plastic hoop earrings. The boy is short, too, but skinny, with sandy hair. His chin juts out, like he's mad at everybody. He has pink plastic things behind each ear, with pink wires that go to a black box hung around his neck and resting on his chest. He marches to the front and sits in one of the empty seats. I wonder why the teacher doesn't make him take his earphones off.

The girl and the woman walk slowly to the front. The girl is tall, with reddish-brown hair and freckles. She has on a baggy green sweater and a brown skirt that almost touches the floor. She looks at the floor when she walks. She can feel the other students' eyes touching her. I can tell. She sits down slowly, beside the woman.

The woman starts to wave her arms around, flicking her hands into funny shapes. She stops, the girl nods, then she starts doing the same thing. I hear a couple of kids snicker and I laugh too.

"Shhhhhh! George, don't!" Hook hisses. "That's rude."

My laugh is cut off. I look at Hook. He has his serious look on. I start to feel bad. I've done something wrong but I don't know what.

Hook leans over. "Those two kids — they have hearing problems," he whispers. "Remember awhile back I told you some more cripples would be coming to the school?"

I try to remember. "Ummmmm . . ."

"Never mind. Doesn't matter. Anyway, the boy there —see that thing around his neck? That's called a 'phonic ear.' It helps him hear, like a radio, by amplifying the sounds and sending them to the earpieces. I heard they might be coming this week."

The teacher is talking to the woman and she and the girl wave their hands around.

"Hook, why do they do that?"

"It's sign language. They can talk that way. It's what you can do if you can't hear. If you're deaf and you can't talk."

The teacher has begun the lesson. He stands at the front, holding the book open on his hand, like a plate. Some students get up and shuffle to the blackboard and start to write numbers and letters. The teacher talks to the woman again.

"How come the girl doesn't have one of those boxes?" I ask Hook.

"I don't think the phonic ear helps you unless you have *some* hearing," he whispers. "I guess the redhead is totally deaf. That's why she uses her hands. I guess that lady is there to help her."

". . . all right, Jesus?" the teacher's voice cuts in.

"Sorry, sir?"

"Would you put your answer to number six on the board, please?"

"Okay." Hook passes his notebook over to me. "Let's hope my answer is right, George."

"Hey, wait, Hook. I don't —"

"No sweat George, just copy it down. You can do it."

I don't like this. I don't want to go up there in front of everybody. Some kids are looking at me already.

"Come on George, up you go." Hook shoves my shoulder gently.

I get to my feet. I swallow hard. I can feel my face getting hot. I force myself to walk up the long row, past the faces turned to look at me, to the front. Now the faces are behind me. The eyes push against me. Two students are at the board, writing fast. I move to a spot where nothing is written yet.

There is nothing to write with. I turn to the teacher. Hook's notebook bangs the chalk ledge and crashes to the floor. Three loose sheets of paper flutter down. Some kids laugh. The teacher looks from the woman to me.

"What's the matter, George?"

I say nothing. My face is hot. My mouth is dry and words can't get out. I feel a droplet of sweat run down my nose. Then I see the redhead girl's hands move. The woman looks at her, then whispers something to the teacher.

He adjusts his wire glasses with one hand. "Need some chalk, George?" He smiles and tosses a piece of chalk to me. It arcs through the air, spinning end over end. I can feel myself flinch. Before I know it, I snatch the chalk out of the air. I bend over and pick up the notebook and gather the loose sheets. But the notebook is closed. How will I find the part I have to write on the board? I will write down the wrong thing and people will laugh again. Hook will get into trouble.

I look down the long row, past the faces, to Hook. His mouth moves, but no sound comes out. He does it again. It's hard to read his lips. "Last page." His mouth shapes the words. "Last page." I turn to the last page in the notebook. It's there. Number six.

I quickly copy down what's there. I am alone at the board now and all the eyes are on my back. The last line is $X = 10$. I put the chalk down carefully on the ledge. Then I let my breath out slowly and turn around.

The teacher is talking to the boy with the box on his chest. The girl is watching me. She looks straight into my eyes, then shakes her head. She points to the board, then holds up one hand, with the fingers spread.

I want to get out of there. I take a step, but she shakes her head again. Holds up her hand in the same way.

I turn and look at what I wrote. $X = 10$. Quickly, I rub out that line with my hand and write $X = 5$.

As I walk quickly past her, she smiles.

The cafeteria is crowded and noisy — rows and rows of students sit at the long tables on red plastic chairs. The big room has a hollow sound — babble of voices, scrape of chairs on the floor, clink of dishes. At a few of the tables, some of the students are playing cards. A teacher I don't know walks up and down, slapping a long ruler against his leg.

"There they are," says Hook. "Let's go meet them."

The woman and the two deaf kids are sitting at a table by themselves. Each one has a tray of food. The boy has his head down, reading a comic as he spoons soup into his mouth.

"Hi," Hook says as I park the chair. "Mind if we sit here?"

The boy ignores us. The redheaded girl stops chewing and looks at the woman.

"I'm Hook. This is George."

"Hello boys. I'm Mrs. Jackson, this is Heather, and that's Tim." She has very white skin and her mouth turns down at the edges.

I sit down and open my lunch bag and unwrap my sandwiches. Peanut butter. Good. I carefully fold the waxed paper, making a square under the sandwiches.

"I see you ordered the mystery meat and murdered vegetables," Hook says.

"Oh, it's not so bad," Mrs. Jackson laughs. Heather keeps her head down but her eyes look up and back down a lot.

"This your first day here?" Hook says to her, but she doesn't see. The woman taps her arm. Hook asks it again.

Heather looks at Hook, then to the woman, then back at Hook. She is shy. I can tell. She puts down her fork and her arms start to fly and her hands flutter. Her mouth moves a bit at the same time. Sometimes she touches her body, sometimes her mouth, sometimes her hands comes together. Sometimes she uses one hand, flicking the fingers quickly.

"Heather says this is her first day here. Up to now, she's been going to a school for the deaf, but she and her parents wanted her to come to a . . ." the woman pauses, ". . . a normal school. She says to tell you she can read your lips."

"Great," says Hook.

The woman goes on. "I'm here for a few weeks to help Heather communicate with her teachers when she wants to ask questions and so on. I'll also help Tim if he needs me."

We eat in silence for a while. Kids begin to filter out of the cafeteria. Some of them lob bunched up lunch bags into the big garbage drums as they walk past. Others carry trays of dishes to the window.

"What's the comic about?" Hook says to the boy. Tim doesn't look up. Hook looks at me, then at Mrs. Jackson. She taps Tim on the arm. He looks at her, then turns a knob on the black box that hangs around his neck.

"Hook is talking to you, Tim," she says.

"What do you want?" he says. His chin juts out. His voice is strange — sort of hollow, like he is talking through his nose.

"Nothing special. Just wondered what you're reading."

"A comic," Tim answers, then he turns the knob again and lowers his head and turns a page.

Mrs. Jackson looks embarrassed. "Tim is sort of a loner," she explains.

Hook leans across the table and taps Tim on the arm. He slaps the comic down and turns the knob again.

"George and I usually play cards in the library after lunch," Hook says. "How about you and Heather play with us? We can play euchre. You need four for that. The library's on the second floor."

"No thanks," says Tim, turning the knob and lowering his head. I can see a crease form on Hook's brow.

Heather's hands fly around.

"Heather says she'd like to," says Mrs. Jackson.

On the way to the elevator I say to Hook, "I don't remember anything about cards, Hook. Will you remind me how to play before Heather gets there?"

Hook laughs. "You don't remember because we've never done it. Now we gotta get there fast and dig up a deck of cards."

9

"There's nothing to be afraid of," Mitzi says again. "The dentist is just going to check your teeth and clean them."

We are walking down a strange street, leaning into the wind. The wind whips Mitzi's hair around her face and her cheeks are red from the cold.

The dentist's office is in a tall, ugly old house. There is a sign on the brown lawn, squeaking as it swings back and forth, punched by the wind. We turn off the street and walk up the narrow sidewalk.

We push through the front door into a small waiting room. It is early morning and we are the only ones here. There are chairs along the walls and a couple of tables with magazines on them in front of a big window. At the far end is a long counter.

"Well . . . I guess I'll be off." Mitzi looks like she wants to stay, but she puts her hand on the door knob.

"See you later," she says.

I sit down and look out the picture window into a parking lot behind the house, watching dead leaves swirl around the cars.

"George?" There is a woman dressed in white standing behind the counter now. "Would you come this way, please?"

She leads me down a short, narrow hall into a tiny room. In the center a big curved chair with thick arms is waiting. There's a little round sink beside it and machines like spider arms with cords hanging from them. Along the wall behind the chair is a counter top with rows of drawers below it.

"Have a seat." She smiles. She is taller than me, and skinny, with long, narrow arms.

I sit down, sliding deep into the chair. It's hard to sit upright, so I give in and lean back, letting the chair hold me. She slips a silver chain around my neck with a big paper towel clipped to it.

"Just lie back and relax," she says, adjusting the headrest. She switches on a big lamp that is attached to the ceiling by a long arm with a hinge in the middle. I hear the quiet whine of a motor and the chair back drops slowly until I'm almost lying down. The light above me stares down like a yellow eye, pinning me.

The woman beside me looks like a long white rectangle. Her face leans over the chair. "Dr. Maitland will be here momentarily." Her face disappears and I hear her feet brushing the carpet.

Her footsteps return after a bit. Then the floor creaks as someone else comes into the room. Another person appears beside me, a big wide guy with thick hairy arms and a round face.

"So you're George, are you?"

"Yes."

"That's fine. I'm just going to examine your teeth,

George, and see if everything is sound and solid."

The big white shape lowers as he sits on a stool behind my head. Quickly he pulls a round tray held by a spider arm over my chest. His hand is wide and strong, with black hairs on the back. He takes two thin, shiny silver tools off the tray. One has a little mirror on the end. The other has a bright, curved hook on it.

I'm starting to get scared. I struggle to sit upright just as he says, "Open, please." He is holding the sharp hook in front of my face.

I lie back and open my mouth. The tools are cold and they have a bitter taste. The mirror clinks against my teeth. The hook digs around, scraping and screeching. My breathing quickens. Spit trickles to the back of my throat and I begin to choke. When I cough the thick fingers take the tools away.

"Having a little trouble, are we?"

I struggle to sit up again. "I . . . I think I better go."

"Nonsense. We've just started. Just try to relax." He turns his face away. "Suction, please."

I hear the woman rummaging around behind the chair. A clear plastic tube appears in front of my face, hook-shaped, with a thin hose attached.

"Open, please."

The tube is hung on my lower teeth and sticks under my tongue. It makes a gurgling noise. I can feel it sucking the spit out of my mouth. The tools glint in the light for a second. More clinking and scraping. It doesn't hurt, though, and I start to relax a little, staring up into the yellow eye.

After a while the tools are taken away and the thick hands drop them on the tray. A voice comes from behind my head.

"You have a cavity, but it's a small one. I can fill it right now."

I do not know what a cavity is. Drawers open and close behind the chair. Then one of the big hands appears.

It's holding a long, long needle. A tiny drop of clear liquid hangs from the point.

"Open, please."

Fingers of the other hand pull my lip away from my gums. The needle jabs way up into my lip, up into my face, under my eye, then the pain begins to go away. The needle stays in there a long time and my face begins to feel funny. The hand with the needle disappears. A finger of the other hand rubs the spot where the needle went in. A tool with a curved hook appears for a second. I feel the cold metal against my lower lip.

"Feel that?" he asks. I hear the tool banging against a tooth.

I can't talk. His hand is still in my mouth. "Uhh, uhh," I say.

"Good. Now, you won't feel this either. I'm just going to drill a little before I put the filling in."

A big hand reaches up and grabs the thin pencil thing on the spider arm above me, pulling it toward my face.

"Open wide."

A hot wave rolls through me. I can feel the sweat trickle from my armpits down to my back and I start to breathe fast again. The plastic tube sucks and gurgles like a feeding insect.

Then I grip the chair arms hard. Holding back. Fighting the terror that swirls around me like black smoke.

Because I can feel myself slipping. Down and down.

A wild, angry buzz comes from my mouth. Grinding and whining on my tooth. The vibration travels along my jaw until my skull buzzes. The noise deafens me, filling my skull, like wind roaring in a black cave.

I am slipping into The Well. I can't stop. In the sky

above me long silver shapes dart from the sky, whining and buzzing. Around me the people scream and run, trying to hide in the trees. But the silver shapes whine closer. Bringing death.

I hear voices I do not recognize drumming against the stone walls of The Well, like fists. I stay still. Slowly, the smoke begins to clear.

I am sitting in a chair. Outside the window, a parking lot filled with cars. Bright sun. There is a tree out there, tall and bare. Branches toss like waves.

Beside me, a woman is talking to a small child. I am in a small room with chairs along the walls. I see my coat hung on a hook by the door.

I stand. Walk across the room. Put on my coat and open the door.

"George, are you feeling all —"

Then the door closes behind me as the cold wind snatches me. A sign on the brown lawn squeaks, swinging in the wind. I walk out to the street. I turn — which way?

I am walking along Elmwood and I can see the school. I go in the gate, up the sidewalk under the bare trees. I am cold. My jaw aches.

I enter the school, walk down the empty hall, turn into the hall where my locker is. There are three kids in this hall. Two guys wearing sweaters with ELMWOOD printed on them. They are laughing and banging around in their lockers. Down the hall is a small black girl, reaching up into her locker. The overhead lights flash on her mirror glasses.

Locker doors slam and the two guys hook the locks on, snap them shut. Suddenly one clouts the other on the head with a book and takes off, laughing, down the hall. The other shouts something and runs after him, fast, feet thundering. The first guy skids around the corner, past the girl. Just as the girl steps back from her locker, arms full of books, the second guy barrels by, smashing into her. The girl's books fly in all directions. Her glasses spring from her head and loop through the air as she falls heavily. The guy keeps running, yelling "Sorry!" as he tears around the corner.

The girl does not get up right away. Just rolls onto her stomach, then struggles to her hands and knees. I walk closer to her, staring.

She is very small, and pretty. Her black skin is not like Bob's. Hers is so black it's almost shiny. She has long, frizzy hair and big gold hoops in her ears. She has on tight jeans and a pink T-shirt.

She starts to crawl around, groping along the floor. Her hands find the mirror glasses, clutch them, put them on quickly. She rises to her knees and brushes the dirt off her arms.

Then she lowers her hands to the floor again. She begins to move in a circle, groping. As she circles, wider each time, she slowly gathers her books. I can hear her now. She is mumbling under her breath. I know the sound — anger mixed with the no-power feeling.

I quickly bend and snatch up the one book she missed.

"Who's there?" she says sharply. "Why don't you watch where you're going!"

"Here," I say, holding out the book. Why is she mad at me? Should I leave?

She stands and holds out her hand for the book. But she does not look at me. The mirror glasses look past me. She moves her arm until her hand hits the book. Then she takes it.

She tucks all the books under one arm and steps toward her locker, one arm held straight out in front of her. When her hand touches the locker beside hers, she gropes first one way then the other until her hand hits the open door. Then she steps closer. She reaches inside the locker.

She takes out a white cane.

"Are you still there?" she snaps as she slams the locker door. She fumbles as she hooks the lock through the catch and closes it.

"Uh, yes."

"You're pretty rude, aren't you?"

"It wasn't me," I stammer. "He's gone. It was someone else."

She turns the mirrors to me. "Yeah, you're right. Your footsteps came from the other direction. Sorry."

"That's okay."

She puts the white cane to the floor and balances it against her stomach, then holds out her hand.

"I'm Amie," she says.

I shake with her. "You can't see, can you?"

"No, but I'm still Amie. Well, who are you?"

"George."

"Glad to meet you, George. I'm a new student. I just started yesterday. I hope those two goons aren't the welcoming committee." She laughs and adds, "How about showing me around? The guidance guy gave me the grand tour yesterday, but I haven't memorized everything yet. That'll take a week or so."

"Sure," I answer. "Come on up to the library. There's someone I want you to meet."

10

The four of us are waiting for the snow.

We have our chairs arranged in an arc in front of the big picture window of the library. It's quiet here at this time of day. The library is on the second story of the school. From here we can see across the track and football field to Elmwood Avenue. On the left is the flat roof of the gym wing, all pipes and vents. On the right is the double row of trees where Hook and I used to eat lunch sometimes before the weather turned cold. The trees are all bare now.

Heather's chair is turned so she can see our faces easily. She is dressed in long, roomy clothes — a baggy shirt, open sweater, a skirt that almost brushes the floor, and leather boots. Hook said one time that she looked like she wore her grandmother's clothes. She answered that she does. And she buys used clothes from the Salvation Army store near her house.

Heather's hands begin to talk.

"Heather says we have Math in ten minutes," I tell Hook.

I am learning how to read Heather's sign language. She has no one to help her because Mrs. Jackson has gone and Tim went back to the deaf school. I understand most of what Heather says. The rest I sort of fill in. Hook gave me the job of learning her signing. That was about a week after he asked her to be the third member of the Cripples' Club. I helped him solve a Math problem one day. Then he got that look he gets when an idea hits him.

"If you can understand this junk," he said, pointing to the Math book, "you can understand Heather. I'm not swift enough, and obviously Amie can't do it. So you're *it*, George."

Hook turns to look at Heather. "Let's skip it today, okay Heather? This is a big day. First snowfall of the year. Also the first snowfall for *us*. *Also*, the first snowfall ever — we think — for George. Anyway, it's the first he remembers, which is the same thing."

Heather smiles and makes the okay sign. Hook is off and running.

"You know, snow is sort of symbolic. It covers everything, no matter how crappy or dirty or ugly, and makes it new and pure again. And for the four of us, it'll be a communion. Right? According to the weatherman, this snowfall will be great."

Outside, there is a stillness. No wind. Not even a little breeze. The sky is low and gray, with a bit of purple in the northwest.

"You see what I mean?" Hook asks.

"No," Amie answers, "I don't."

We all laugh, Amie the loudest. This is a joke she makes a lot.

She is wearing tight red cords and a bright yellow T-shirt. Her mirror glasses cover a lot of her face. She never takes them off. Hook says a lot of blind people wear sunglasses so you can't see their eyes.

She is a year older than me, and smarter than all the rest of us put together. You can pick her out a mile away — the mirror glasses, the white cane, and her portable computer. It fits in a case like the ones the teachers carry.

It was Amie's idea to make the library our regular meeting place. She spends a lot of time here. She takes three subjects on individual study because she's way ahead of the other kids.

Outside, the snow has begun. Small icy flakes just sort of *appear* in the air, then fall slowly, straight to earth. We watch, saying nothing. I have never seen anything this strange. Soon there is a silvery coating, like paint, on all the cars, sidewalks, and the driveway — even the grass on the football field.

Then the snow thickens. The flakes are fat, dropping arrow-straight, like millions of tiny elevators. We can't see Elmwood Avenue now. The snow piles up fast and all the shapes — the pipes and vents on the roof, the cars, the fences — get rounded and white and soft.

"Yeah. Everything new again," Hook says quietly.

He does this a lot. I mean, he sees things behind things. Like all this thinking about the snow, what it *means*. Hook is an average student, but he sees things differently, things that other people don't see.

I am enjoying the snow. Sitting relaxed, taking it all in. It's amazing to me. Things don't disappear like I thought they might. But suddenly they're not the same.

After a while the snow lets up and falls more gently. There is a white world on the other side of the glass with not a mark on it.

Then from the parking lot a figure appears, walking toward the main doors. From up here we can see the footprints, like the person is a pencil point, drawing a crooked pencil line across the snow. As the figure comes nearer, we can see it's dressed in black. There is snow on his head and shoulders.

"It's old Silverheels," Hook says as the black figure passes below us. "Wonder what he's up to."

Heather's hands start talking. "Why doesn't the school expel that jerk? Everybody knows he's bad news." I pass it on.

"Evidence," Hook answers. "My uncle says the office knows he and his bunch run a protection scheme —"

"A what?" Amie asks.

"Protection. He and his friends pick out a certain number of kids every year, one for each of them. All niners, all with spending money. They beat one of them up. Then they make the rest pay *not* to be beaten up. Simple. If one of the niners goes to the office or the cops, he *really* gets it."

"Nice guys," Amie says.

"Yeah, well, wait 'til you hear side B. They also sell drugs. They set up the business in this school, but they never deal on school property. My uncle says Silverheels is a smart guy and he has his organization set up to protect himself. The cops have nailed one or two of the gang, but never him. He's over eighteen, but he hasn't graduated because — now get this — he needs one more credit. The school would love him to graduate and go away. Far away. But he stays on the roll, flunks all his courses, and legally the school has to let him come.

"He's kind of a sad case, in a way," Hook adds after a moment. "His dad used to beat him up when he was a kid. Now the old man's gone. And his mother drinks. No wonder."

I look down at the gray trail Silverheels has cut through the white snow.

"Why does he bother with school at all?" I ask.

"Well, for one thing, this is where his gang is, and he needs them."

Amie cuts in. "And his market is here, right?"

"Right. A lot of it, anyway. And he is a pretty wealthy guy now."

Amie leans back in her chair and turns the mirrors to the ceiling. We can almost *hear* her thinking.

"This is not a big problem folks. There are three ways to get out of school, right? You can quit, get thrown out, or graduate."

"What's Amie saying?" Heather's hands ask, and I pass on the message.

"Sorry, Heather, I forgot."

Amie means she forgot Heather can't see her lips move if she's facing the ceiling. She repeats what she said and then goes on.

"We know Silverheels won't quit. And he's too crafty to get expelled. You said there's no evidence against him. Do you guys remember Sherlock Holmes?"

"Yeah, the English detective," Heather answers. "But what's *he* got to do with this?"

After I translate, Amie says, "Sherlock said many times, if you eliminate all possibilities but one, then that one must be the solution, no matter how unlikely it seems."

Hook rolls his eyes. "Well, thanks a lot for making it clear!" he groans.

Amie smiles and whispers, "So let's make sure he graduates!"

The three of us look at each other for a few seconds. Outside, the snow is still coming down gently, and there's a little breeze.

"I don't get it," Heather signs.

I don't get it either, but I say nothing.

"Okay," Amie announces, "let's hit the elevator."

Still confused, we get up and leave the library. There are

big double doors on either end of the room, with crash
bars on them. I push Hook out one way and the girls go
out the other. From the back, they look strange, almost
funny. A small kid with a grownup's case and a tall
redhead with granny clothes on.

A few minutes later we are in the elevator, stopped
between floors.

Hook and Amie have legal keys for the elevator. Back in
November, when the Cripples' Club grew to four
members, I took his key to the hardware store and got
copies made for Heather and me.

We use the elevator for conferences when we don't want
anyone to hear us. And for when one of us gets a *syntax
error*. That's Amie's term. She says it's computer talk for
when there's something wrong in a program. The
program gets all tangled up and stops running and *syntax
error* shows on the screen. So if one of us gets really mad or
upset or something, that's a *syntax error* and the elevator
is where we go. We stop it between floors and stay in there
until we feel calm. It's private — the only private place in
the school.

I've been in here twice — I think twice — when I felt
myself slipping into The Well. But I never come in here
alone — that would be worse.

"Hook," Amie is saying, "you know where the computer terminal is in the Guidance Office?"

"Sure, but —"

"Roll down there and see if you can get close to the
terminal. Probably you'll find a phone number and a
code. The code will be a few letters or numbers or both.
Most computer operators write them down, then tape
them to the desk top or somewhere close. Maybe inside a
drawer. If you find them, come back here with them."

Hook pushes a button and the elevator starts down.

"Let's go, George."

Ten minutes later, we are back in the elevator. Hook gives Amie a small piece of paper with ELMW copied onto it.

"No phone number," he says.

"Dammit."

"What's the problem?" Heather signs. "Why do we need the school phone number? And even if we do, it will be in the phone book. Probably listed under *Boring Places*."

"It's not the school number we need," Amie says after I have passed on the message. "It's the special number that gets us into the Board of Education's computer. The code gets us into Elmwood's records, which are stored in the computer's memory. If we were using the terminal in that office, we could get in directly, but from here we need the computer's telephone linkage number."

I still don't know what Amie's up to. All this computer talk means almost nothing to me. But Hook sees it. A big, sly smile spreads slowly across his face. He taps his hook to his head and nods toward Amie.

"Well," she goes on, "I guess we'll have to do it the hard way."

She sits down on Hook's knee and rests her feet on top of his as he groans, "Ooofff! What an elephant!"

"Somebody help me unpack Siggy."

Siggy is her portable computer. She named him after some doctor who, according to her, was an important psychologist. She says he was one of the first people to really understand how people's minds work. She's read most of what this doctor wrote. Siggy is about the size of a portable typewriter, flat on top and bottom, like an oversized book. Amie explained to me one time that Siggy runs on batteries. The batteries keep his RAM alive when she turns him off. I still do not know what all that means, but I don't tell her that.

Heather plunks Siggy onto Amie's knee. Amie works fast, snapping the catches and flipping up the light gray lid. The underside of the lid is the screen. The rest is the keyboard. Heather takes another piece out of the case and puts it on the floor. She puts the end of the wire into Amie's hand and Amie feels along Siggy's side and plugs the wire in. Heather hands her a stack of diskettes.

After turning Siggy on, Amie takes the diskettes and feels the paper covers with her fingertips until she finds the one she wants. She's reading the Braille titles. She slides the diskette into a slot in Siggy's side. Then she types RUN PHONELIST. After a little humming sound some writing comes on the screen and Amie says, "It will save time if you read for me, George. Siggy will print out the screen contents in Braille for me but it takes time. Okay, here goes."

She types BOARD ED and the disk spins again.

"Got it," I tell her. "777-3434."

"Okay, dial it, please, Heather, and then give me the phone. You folks are about to hear an Oscar performance."

"Not me," say Heather's hands. After I translate, everyone laughs.

The elevator has a phone beside the door for emergencies. Lucky for us, it isn't just an extension. We can phone outside. Heather dials the number and puts the phone into Amie's hand.

Amie clears her throat. "Okay, folks. No giggles. Promise?"

She turns her face up. The lights reflect in her mirrors. She clears her throat, then lowers her head.

"Yes, hello. To whom am I speaking? I see. Perhaps you can help me."

The voice Hook and I hear isn't Amie's, but it's coming out of her mouth. It's deep, like an older woman who smokes too much. I quickly mouth this to Heather.

Amie continues. "This is Scott of Bell Systems Computer Linkage calling. I'm running a check on all our customers who use more than fifty KPT's per month for computer linkages. Yes. Now, your computer linkage number is 777-3434, is that correct? . . . Oh, of course. That's the number I just dialed, isn't it? How silly of me. I read from the wrong line. What was that again?"

While she talks, with the phone jammed between her skinny shoulder and frizzy black hair, she types 777-6868.

"Good. Now, then, any problems? . . . I shouldn't? Ah, to whom *should* I speak, then? Yes, I have it. I'll call him immediately. Thank you. Sorry to trouble you. Goodbye."

She holds out the phone, puffing her cheeks and blowing the air out slowly, with relief. Heather takes the phone and hangs up.

"Hey," Hook says from behind Amie's back, "what the hell's a KPT?"

"Search me. I just made that up."

We all laugh again. Even Heather. When she laughs, her mouth opens and we hear a sort of *hiss, hiss, hiss.* Sometimes we laugh at her laugh and that gets her going even more.

But right now we are too busy, and too interested in what Amie's doing.

"Okay, Heather, attach the phone to the modem and dial 777-6868." She means the part that Heather put on the floor and Amie plugged into Siggy's side.

Heather makes the connection and soon we hear a high *beep!* from the modem.

"Okay, we're in," Amie announces. "We are now talking directly to the Board of Ed's computer. What's Silverheels's real name, Hook?"

"Kevin Ross," he says to the back of her head. "Hey,

fatso. How about shifting your buns a little?"

"Why?" she asks as her fingers fly. "Am I turning you on?"

"Absolutely. But I'd also like to see Siggy. It's getting boring back here. And besides, you've got dirt behind your ears and it looks gross. That's better," he adds as Amie shifts.

While those two type and talk, Amie speaking to Siggy through her fingers and Hook telling her what Siggy says on the screen, I mouth silently to Heather, "Do you know what Amie's doing?"

Heather signs back, "Maybe Silverheels will graduate before he thinks."

"Absolutely beautiful!" Hook sings. "Old Silverheels got forty-five percent in grade twelve English. His teacher was Ball and —"

"*Bald?*" Amie cuts in. "Is *that* what it says?"

"No, Dummie. Ball. You know, what soccer players kick around?"

"Heather wants to know who you're calling a dummie," I say.

Amie starts to go into her Giggle when she hears this. If she really gets going, she'll go out of control. Hook slips his hook through one of Amie's gold hoops and tugs.

"Ow!" she yells. "Hands off!" Now we all start to laugh.

Then serious again. "Ball," says Amie. "No teacher by that name at this school now, right?"

"Right."

"Perfect. Then nobody can ask Ball if he goofed. We'll make it look like a typing error. Tell me when the cursor is under the four."

She taps a key again and again until Hook says to stop. Then she types *54.*

Heather claps twice and makes the okay sign.

"Silverheels just passed grade twelve English. Which was . . . how many years ago?"

"Three," I answer. The dates are on the screen.

"Right. And when the end of January rolls around and the semester ends, Guidance will ask the computer to do a credit count and will discover that Silverheels has enough to graduate."

"You really think this will work?" Hook asks.

"Maybe not, but it's worth a try," Amie answers.

"Bye-bye to the slime ball," says Hook through his teeth as Heather hangs up the phone. "Absolutely."

"Right on!" say Heather's hands.

The halls are crowded as we make our way back to the library. It's a class change. Kids shout and bang locker doors. The crowd parts around Amie and flows past her. It would be easier if one of us could lead her when it's this crowded but she never lets us. I keep bumping Hook's chair into people by accident. I'm thinking hard.

When we get back to our chairs at the windows the snow has stopped. Footprints dot the driveway and sidewalks.

Heather's hands are talking. "I've got to get to class. We already missed Math."

"No, wait," I hear myself saying.

They all look surprised. I say, "Amie, can you get into anybody's computer?"

"No. Only the ones with weak defense systems. Banks and stock brokers and government computers are really hard to crack. Even if you can get a code like we did today, it's almost impossible."

"What about a church?"

"A church? They don't have computers, George."

"No, I mean the main office of a church. Like the United Church of Canada."

"They may not even have one. They may share space in someone else's. It's hard to say. Why? What's up, George?"

"Hey, George, that's not a bad idea," Hook cuts in. "Absolutely!"

Heather is asking what we're talking about. Before I can answer, Hook says, "George wants to find out who he is and where he came from. Maybe the people who brought him from Hong Kong store this information about him —the information that they won't give out — in a computer file."

"Yeah, right," Amie says. "And if they do, maybe Siggy can do a little secret research."

Heather looks at me. Real serious. She knows about me. They all do.

Her hands ask me slowly, "Are you *sure* you want to do this, George?"

I don't translate for the others. I look at each of their faces. I know they'll help me when it gets tough. Not *if.* *When.*

"Yes, I want to. I *have* to."

"Okay," says Hook. "Gather round."

We make a circle around his chair and join hands. This was Heather's idea, the hand holding.

"The next project of the Cripples' Club is hereby begun, and we solemnly dedicate ourselves to it."

One by one we say, *Amen.* As Amie speaks, she squeezes my hand a little.

11

Even though it's cold out today, with an icy wind, I decide to walk back to school the long way, past Amie's house. I have been home for lunch. I go home for lunch on the days when Hook is at physio, what he calls the torture chamber. It's good to get away from the school for a while.

The long way goes through Robinsons' Bush, which is a long, narrow piece of land with no houses. The kids call it Robinsons' Bush because that's the name of the family who used to own all the land around here when it was all farms. There is a small creek that twists through the area and the trees follow the creek. Heather told me the city won't allow the land to be used for houses.

This is a quiet street, with big houses set far back from the road in big yards. You hardly ever see people walking and only a few cars pass up and down. This is why I like to go back to school this way. It's peaceful and I can think about things.

The street feels lonely today. Piles of dirty snow, plowed from the road, line the curbs. The dull sky seems to come right down to the sidewalk. There is no one around except another person walking far ahead of me.

Suddenly I realize it's Amie. She moves slowly, feeling ahead with her cane for patches of ice on the sidewalk. Siggy is with her. I begin to walk faster to catch up with her.

Up ahead of her the frozen creek passes under the road, through one of those monster pipes, big enough to walk through. The bare trees come almost to the road there.

After she passes the creek, three dark figures separate from the evergreens behind her. They move up to her. All four figures stop for a second, then cut away from the sidewalk into the trees.

There is something wrong. Siggy has been left behind on the sidewalk and Amie's cane lies in the snow.

I start to run.

Her cane is lying beside the computer. I peer through the trees. There are evergreens mixed thick with the bare trunks of maples. I can't see anyone. But there is a scuffle of prints in the powdery snow.

I follow the prints carefully, quietly.

They are there, not far in from the street, but out of sight. I creep silently behind a big evergreen and squint between the broad sprays of the branches. There is no wind in the bush, and no noise.

Amie is being held by two Black Ones against a chain-link fence that follows the lip of the small gully where the creek lies frozen. They are good at what they're doing. She is pinned, helpless. On each side a Black One has a leg wedged between hers and holds one of her arms up beside her head, pressing his weight into the fence. From this angle, behind and to the side, I can see her down coat is unzipped. The third Black One has jammed her scarf into her mouth and holds it there with one hand. His other hand is inside her coat. The bare black branches reflect in her upturned mirror glasses.

I have to concentrate hard to calm my mind, to clear away the anger. I breathe slowly, with long breaths, because my heart is hammering. As I slip off my coat, I realize they are whispering. They sound like ghosts in the quiet bush.

"Every week," one is saying. "This will happen *some*where, *some*time, *every* week."

"Unless you pay," hisses another voice. "Fifteen a week, five for each of us. Understand?"

Amie's head jerks up and down. She groans. Her breath escapes her nostrils in sharp, frosty puffs.

"Unless," the one holding her mouth mocks her, "unless you *like* this." Inside her coat, his hand moves.

I close the distance between us with two quick strides. Coming behind the one who just spoke, I slap my hands hard against the sides of his head, against his ears. As a yelp of pain explodes from him, I sweep his feet out from under him with a low circling kick. He drops to the ground with a heavy grunt. I hear his head thud into the snow.

Surprised, the other two have not reacted. I pivot on my left foot, snapping a roundhouse kick into the ribcage of the Black One on Amie's right. I use a roundhouse because I have to kick over the body of the fallen one. I aim the kick into his kidney. It's a good kick — I can tell by the feel — but the ribs don't break. The pain will put him out of action. He drops, silent, to his knees, one hand clutching the chain links for balance, the other where the kick landed. He tries to breathe.

The third has had time to get ready, but only a few seconds. He has let go of Amie and stepped to the side of the first one. He looks down at his friends, then toward the street. He wants to run, but wants to be loyal. I decide for him, moving to the side to cut off his escape. I move toward him through the snow on smooth, gliding steps.

He hunches over, fists up. He's experienced. I make a couple of feints with my forward fist and he reacts. He aims a punch at my face. I block it smoothly, knocking it above my head. For a split second, before he uses his second fist, his whole body is exposed. I glide into him, putting him off balance, and snap three quick, piercing punches — throat, stomach, groin. I glide back, before he can react. But he is helpless now, doubled over, ready to fall like his friend kneeling at the fence. I sweep his feet away and he drops like a log.

Amie is rigid against the fence, the scarf still in her mouth. She is too terrified to scream.

"Amie!" I urge her. "It's okay. I'm here, now. It's okay."

The scarf falls away.

"George? Is it you? Oh, thank God. Is it really you, George?"

"Yes. Stay where you are, Amie. I'll get you out of here in a minute."

The first Black One is getting up, slapping snow from his leather jacket. His shock is under control now. He is shaking his head.

"You dirty little chink." His voice is full of hate. He has forgotten to whisper. He wipes wet snow from his cheek, smearing a dirty line there. He spits.

"Let's see how your scummy chink fighting works when you can't sneak up behind someone."

For the first time ever, I want to hurt somebody. I can feel the hate burning in me, white hot, sparking and popping. Because I can see a picture in my mind of Amie forced against the fence, helpless, with whispers knifing at her from the darkness. And a hand creeping like a slug under her sweater.

We are taught to fight silently, without hate, without fear. *Shīfu* always talks to us about this. "Use your skill to defend," he repeats. "Do not seek conflict. Choose to run away if fighting can be avoided. Fight only to end fighting. Don't punish."

But now I want to punish, and the want takes me over.

The Black One taunts me. "Come on, scum. Come on."

So I strike first. I kick him on his left thigh, beside the crotch. Close. My foot leaves a wet mark on the cloth.

"Missed," he sneers.

Then again, this time on the right thigh. He tries to counter punch, but misses. I land a light kick above his crotch.

By now he has got the message. He begins to look worried.

Changing to a hand attack, I go for his face, using an open hand. *Slap!* to his right cheek. *Slap!* to his left. He tries to block but most strikes get through. Only one or two of his weak counter punches land. Then he quits trying. All his attention is given to blocking my hits.

Slap! again, harder. *Tap!* on his nose with a back fist. Then another back fist, with a little more power. His nose begins to bleed. His eyes water.

I put a light kick into his crotch. This one hurts a little, but he's still standing. His right hand drops to his crotch. *Slap! Slap! Slap!* to his right cheek. Up comes the hand. Another sharp kick to his crotch.

He is helpless, now, moaning with frustration. I step into him, swatting his arms away, grabbing his hair and pulling his face down to my level. His face is wet with melted snow, mud, blood, and water from his eyes.

"You know who we are, don't you, the four of us?" I say it real calm.

"Y - yes."

"Tell them," I say. "Tell them all. Leave us alone. We are protected. Understand?"

"Yeah."

I let him go, pushing him aside. I step over to Amie. She flinches as I zip up her down coat and wrap her scarf around her neck. All the time I'm talking to her, reassuring her.

Behind me, the others are sneaking away silently. I lead Amie to where I dropped my jacket. I suddenly feel cold. I begin to shake a little from cold, excitement, and from the hate cooling and draining away. I realize that I am barefoot. My boots and socks lie under my jacket.

When we step out of the bush the street is empty.

"Let's get you home," I say, picking up her things.

Her voice tells me she has regained some control. "No," she answers. "To school."

"Do you think that's a good idea? You've had a shock and —"

"If I go home, Eleanor will bombard me with a million questions. And I don't want her to know about this." Eleanor is the housekeeper.

I think I see what she means. "Okay."

"*Nobody* can know about this, George. *Nobody*. Not even the others. Promise me!"

"Sure. I promise."

We walk slowly toward the school. The bush on either side of us is quiet. A car swooshes past, throwing slush.

"Promise me, George."

I turn and see she is crying silently. I put down Siggy and her cane and put my arms around her. She hugs me fiercely. We stand like this for a minute in the cold.

Then we start walking again. We will enter the school and head for the elevator. I will pick up a couple of Cokes from the pop machine near the gym.

We will be in the elevator a long time.

12

I am late arriving at Amie's house because I had to shovel out the driveway at home before I could leave. It is still snowing gently, not too cold out. Mitzi said this morning it was perfect weather for Christmas Day.

I knock on Amie's big front door and Eleanor lets me in, saying, "Merry Christmas, George." She is a small, older woman, my height and very thin. She always wears her hair pinned up in a bun on top of her head, and always wears an apron. Eleanor often seems to be grouchy but she isn't. Her kindness glows behind the hard words. She takes care of Amie when her father is away, which is most of the time. He's an airline pilot.

Amie's house is big inside. The living room has thick carpets, dark furniture, and heavy brass lamps. There is a small plastic Christmas tree in the corner with opened packages underneath. It looks lonely in the huge room, as if it is waiting for something.

Our house is not like this. It's on a street where lots of little houses are packed close together. Inside, the rooms are small, too. It has no second floor.

We had a great Christmas. Last night Bob, Mitzi, and I went for a walk in the snow after Bob got home from work. We looked at all the lights strung on the houses and trees. Then we went back and had beef stroganoff. Bob and Mitzi had a bottle of wine with dinner. Then we put our presents under the huge tree — the top scraped the ceiling — that Bob bought from the Boy Scouts. Before we went to bed we watched *A Christmas Carol* on TV.

In the morning I got them up early and we opened the presents. I gave Bob a wool scarf, and Mitzi a brooch. I got a new *Shàolín* suit.

That was this morning. This afternoon is the official Cripples' Club Christmas.

Eleanor tells me to go on up to Amie's rooms. When I walk in I hear them shout, "Merry Christmas, George!" Then one voice saying, "Absolutely!"

They are all there. Hook is in his chair, dressed in a Santa suit but without the beard. He says "Ho, ho, ho!" every few minutes. Heather is on the couch, sipping a ginger ale. She has a new haircut, short, and her freckles stand out more than ever under her blue eyes. She's wearing a baggy dress, pulled in at the waist with a wide leather belt. Amie has a new pair of gold hoops, bigger than ever, and is wearing a snow-white jump suit.

Amie has two rooms. This one has a couch, sound system, and a double desk jammed with computer equipment. One wall is solid bookshelves, packed with thick books — Braille books are a lot thicker than normal. Above the couch is a picture window and outside, above my three friends' heads, I can see the snow falling.

Through an open door I can see Amie's bed, with a crucifix on the wall. Amie is very religious.

Amie's rooms are different from ours. There are no lamps, just a single light on the ceiling. "People like me save a lot of money on electricity," she told us one time. She doesn't turn on the light unless she has company. The whole place is neat and tidy — that's the only way she can find things. The furniture is always in exactly the same place.

There is Christmas music coming from the two big speakers on either side of the couch. Heather sits with her hand, palm down, on one of the speakers. She says she can feel the music. There is lots of pop, candy, chips, and fruit on the table in front of the couch.

We sit and talk for a while, telling what presents we got, making jokes, kidding each other.

Then after a little silence Heather's hands say, "The best present I ever got was to meet you three."

Hook and Amie make quiet noises of agreement, sort of embarrassed. Heather continues talking through me, slowly, because the stuff she wants to say isn't familiar to me and it's hard to translate some of her signs. In the background the Christmas songs fill the pauses while her hands move.

"I want to say this," she continues, "because it's important. Before, even at the school where I learned to sign, I felt *alone* most of the time. Everybody around me had the same problem, more or less, so the whole school was set up for us. There were no normal kids there. You felt like you were living in a big cocoon, with miles of cotton padding insulating you from the rest of the world. It was a different kind of aloneness, you know?

"But now I feel like I'm making it in the real world. The Club helps me be . . . be, I don't know, be *me*. Yeah, that's it. In the other school, I never felt like the real me. Now I do. That's all."

She reaches over to get a paper-wrapped candy from the

table and takes a long time to unwrap it. In the silence that follows I look at Hook. His brown eyes are as bright as the lights Bob put on our Christmas tree. They are over-flowing with happiness at what Heather's hands have said. And I remember for the thousandth time that all this was his idea, that most of the things we did came from him. And I wonder for the thousandth time what we would do without him. We would all lead separate, lonely lives.

"Well," Amie breaks the silence, "I think what Heather said is a great introduction for George's gift."

"Yeah," Hook says.

"What gift? What do you mean?" For a second I'm afraid that I have forgotten something, that maybe we were all supposed to buy presents for each other and it slipped my mind.

But Amie has already got up and moved to the long computer table. When she walks around in her room you would never know she is blind, except she moves a little slower than what she calls "sighted" people.

She flips some switches and little lights blink on. She snaps the phone receiver into a modem.

As she sits down in front of the keyboard Hook says, "Wait, Amie. Remember our agreement?"

Amie turns the swivel chair to face the couch. "Yeah, okay. Heather, you ask, okay?"

Heather's eyes look straight into mine. Her hands say, "Remember a month or so ago you asked Amie to do something for you? Something about finding some infor-mation?" She smiles.

I can feel a wave break over me. All day — since yesterday, in fact — I've had a strange feeling, really strange, that something *big* was going to happen. I couldn't name the feeling, but it's been there, like the knot in your stomach when you're waiting for something important. At first I thought it was just being keyed up about my first Christmas, but the feeling stayed after this morning when we opened our gifts.

My voice swells in my throat. "Yeah, I remember. Why? What did you find out, Amie?"

"Wait," say the hands. "Amie doesn't know what she found, exactly. She *thinks* it may be something. But first we want you to think, George. You said Bob told you that if you find out who you are, where you come from, it might be painful. It might be hard."

Over Heather's head I can see out the window. The snow is still falling, but a wind has come up and the flakes swirl against the glass.

"So we want you to be sure this is what you want."

My three friends are looking at me as if I might suddenly disappear. How can I explain that my answer *has* to be yes? That if you don't know who you *were* you don't know who you *are*?

So I just say, "Yes, it's what I want."

Hook runs his left hand through his black curls. He does that when he's nervous. "Okay, but don't jump ahead of things, George. Maybe Amie got nothing. We don't know. Only you can tell that. This *may* be a big disappointment."

Heather arranges two chairs around Amie and Hook rolls over to the desk. On a shelf up above the computer is a portable TV. It doesn't belong there. Amie doesn't use a monitor. It has been hooked up just for today.

"Okay, George," says Amie. "I want to take you through this step by step, so you'll see what I've been up to. It will take some time, so hang on."

"I'll hang on."

She turns the chair to the table. "Problem one. Does this organization — the United Church — store its files on a computer? To find out, I do this."

She carefully punches a number into the phone. A second or two later the monitor glows. On a red background, a big word in black: COMPUPAC.

"I subscribe to a computer data base system which I can access by phone. It's in the city. So I get to their social services catalogue. Like this."

I don't follow all the big words too well, but I say nothing. I don't want her to stop and explain.

She types for a second and the screen shows a list of clubs and organizations. I can see the one we want there, with an address and a phone number.

The ones that you can talk to by computer should have an asterisk beside them," says Amie.

"Absolutely," Hook puts in. "There's one there."

"Okay," continues Amie. "Dial the number, somebody."

Heather stabs at the phone with her finger. She couldn't have seen what Amie said, so I know they've rehearsed this. The screen goes blank, then lights up again. It shows a list of things you can choose: sending electronic mail to the organization, checking out coming events, other stuff. At the bottom of the screen it says, FOR FURTHER ACCESS, USE YOUR PASSWORD.

"Looks like a dead end," Hook says dramatically.

Amie has been fingering — reading — the print-out. She has a printer beside the keyboard that chatters and whines like a squirrel. It prints in Braille what we see on the screen. She finds what she wants.

"Now, we go into the computer and find the Church's organizations around the world. We don't need a password for that."

She types for a bit. "See it up there? Hong Kong. It should say *1259B Nathan Road, Kowloon*. Right?"

"Yes," I say to her back. My voice croaks out over a dry throat.

"But," she continues, "there's no phone number. So. Let that be for a sec."

She breaks the phone connection and dials COMPUPAC again, then rattles away on the keyboard. She has a lot of stuff memorized, so she doesn't need to get a print-out every time. A bunch of colors splash onto the screen and it takes me a minute to tell that it's a city map, showing a big peninsula in yellow, some blue for water, and a big island. The peninsula and the island have lines criss-crossing them and colored dots on them.

"That peninsula is Kowloon," Hook points out. "The island is Hong Kong. But the whole place is usually just called Hong Kong."

Heather stands and traces a line with her finger through the middle of the peninsula.

"And that's Nathan Road," Hook says.

Amie swivels in her chair to face us. Her gold hoops swing. I can see our three faces in her mirror glasses. "Next problem. How do we get the phone number of the computer in Hong Kong?"

"Why not just ask Hong Kong information over the phone?" I cut in. I am getting a little impatient.

"Because they'd give you the number of the organization's main switchboard, not the computer line. Remember, organizations don't advertise their computer linkage numbers. They're sort of secret. So, I *did* ask information for the Church's social service office there to —"

"Wait," I interrupt again. "You just said —"

"Hang on, George. She'll explain." This comes from Hook.

"— to get the first three digits of the phone number," Amie continues. "I figured the computer access number has the same first three digits."

"You know," Hook adds, "like all our phone numbers begin with 728 or 726."

I nod my head.

Amie says, "Then I only had to find the last four digits. See?"

Above her head the map glows. Nathan Road is a long straight line that cuts the peninsula in two, running right to the blue part. Was I ever in that place?

"Okay, George," Amie says, "we are now at the point where we need to find the last four digits of a phone number. Sounds hard, but it isn't. I wrote a program for Siggy that would generate all the possible combinations for the four digits. Sooner or later, the right combination would turn up. So Siggy would generate a phone number, then try it out over the modem. If a computer didn't answer, Siggy would cut the line immediately, then generate a new number and try again. When a voice answers the phone, or if there *is* no answer within ten rings, it can't be a computer at the other end, because a computer never sleeps and it always answers after a couple of rings.

"With four digits, there are ten thousand possible combinations. If Siggy takes, say, ten seconds to try each call, that's only twenty-seven hours, maximum. So I started the program going and let it run. And Siggy found the number we want!"

I jump out of my chair. "Great! Amie, that's —"

"But," she holds up her right index finger. "I didn't get anything useful out of that computer."

I slump back into my chair and groan. Why is she torturing me like this?

"Because the file has been transferred to Canada. So don't feel bad, George. There's still hope. Watch."

She turns her mirrors to Heather. "Heather, dial the United Church number in the city again, please." Then she swivels back around to face the keyboard.

The map disappears, then the United Church logo

appears, with that same message, FOR FURTHER ACCESS, USE YOUR PASSWORD.

"Now here's the trick, George," Amie says over her shoulder. "It was a real long shot, but it works."

She types PASSWORD, then the telephone number Siggy found for the Hong Kong computer. The screen clears and fills up with print again. It's another menu of choices.

Amie swivels. "I took a chance that the computer in the city would accept the Hong Kong number as a password. And it did!"

"Is this kid a brain, or what? Absolutely!" says Hook.

"Next problem. How to find you in the files. *If* you're there. First, you see on the screen where it says 'Foster Children'? That's you."

Swivel. Rattle of the keyboard. New screen. Swivel again.

"Okay. We got the foster children section of the files, all listed under sex, birthdate, city of origin, etc."

Amie is talking faster now. We're getting near the end. Hook is tapping the tubes of his chair arm with his hook. Heather fidgets in her chair.

"But notice," Amie continues. She points back over her shoulder to the monitor. "There's a last category."

I read. The last category is REFUGEE SPONSORSHIP PROGRAM. I feel cold all of a sudden.

Swivel. Type. Another menu on the screen.

I am very sick of staring at that screen, hoping every change will show me something besides lists and numbers. My neck is cramped from staring upward.

Amie swivels once more. Her gold hoops swing again. "Finally, I found three kids about your age who might be you, George. You know, considering your approximate age, and approximately how long you've been in Canada — stuff like that. But two were girls. So," she pauses for a second, "I'm going to show you the file that *might* be yours. There's not much in it, but let's take a look."

She doesn't swivel this time, but turns slowly.

And types slowly.

And turns again.

I can see the three of us reflected in her mirrors again. Two are looking up. I raise my eyes to the screen.

It is only half filled. With small print.

REFUGEE NUMBER HK1986M15

ORIGIN believed S.E. Asia

DESCRIPTION male, oriental, adolescent, 5'6''

NAME unknown, given: GEORGE

DESTINATION United Church Head Office, Canada

CDN PASSPORT NUMBER FB 587608

CIRCUMSTANCES This young man was picked up off Stonecutters' Island, Hong Kong, the only known survivor of a shipwreck caused by a minor typhoon. Ship originated S.E. Asia. Number of recovered bodies suggests overcrowding of the vessel, of which no trace remains. H.K. Hospital contacted the Church. When found, the boy had a plastic envelope on a string around his neck — as did almost all the bodies recovered — containing what are believed to be travel papers. Most of the document is illegible, except for what may be a surname which in English spelling would be MA. (It was decided to leave the name George, considering the boy's destination.)

"That's all there is, George," says Hook softly.

I am still staring at the screen. I am empty. Everything has been drained away.

Is it me? I wonder. Are those few words *me*?

Hook is talking again. "Remember your dream, George? There's a ship in it, isn't there? And a storm.

And . . ." he pauses a second, to take a slow breath, ". . . and people drowning?"

The room is quiet, except for the Christmas music in the background. A blip of fear crosses the back of my mind. I begin to see bits and pieces of pictures. A dark sky. A ship battered by tall waves. Thin arms reaching above the tossing water.

Hook is talking again. Something about a library, a dictionary. A Chinese/English dictionary. In my mind I can hear the wind, now, howling like a suffering animal.

Hook taps me on the knee with his hook. "George?" He unfolds a piece of paper.

". . . and I found a name, Ma, in the list of Chinese surnames. I photocopied the Chinese character." He hands me the paper.

"Merry Christmas, George," he says. "I hope it means something."

On the paper I see

"Horse," I hear myself saying. "It means Horse." In my mind, the sound of the wind's howling gets louder. I feel my hand squeeze shut on the paper as I begin to slide into The Well, deeper than I've ever been before.

13

"Come on, George, stay with us!"

"The music! George, listen to the Christmas music. Concentrate!"

The voices follow me into The Well. They are like flashlight beams, moving around in the darkness. I feel myself sinking more slowly.

"Come on, George. Don't give in to it. Fight it. Stay with us."

I am coming back now, climbing to the surface on the voice beams. Slowly moving toward the light. I can see a face, a face with freckles and blue eyes. Heather's face.

I am sitting on the couch in Amie's room. I know that. I remember.

"How long have I been out?" I say. I look at my friends. They are scared.

"Only a few minutes," Hook replies. "You came back really fast, George. Absolutely."

Amie is sitting on the swivel chair and above her the monitor glows. The writing is gone, though.

Heather pops open a Coke and hands it to me. Then her hands say, "We made a mistake, didn't we? We shouldn't have told you."

"No, Heather. I'm glad." I unscrunch the little ball of paper in my hand. "I know my name now. And where I came from."

Hook smiles with relief. "Did you mean it? Is your name really *Horse*?"

"Yes, Hook. It's my surname. I'm Chinese. I wasn't born in China, but my parents were Chinese."

Amie says, quietly, "*Were*, George?"

"They're dead, Amie. My mother died when I was a little kid. I didn't really know her. At least I don't think I did. My father . . . no, wait. Maybe he isn't dead. I'm sure he wasn't on the ship."

Heather's hands start to fly. I can hardly keep up with her. "I'm mixed up. You're Chinese but you didn't live in China. What's this *ship* thing all about? And what about all that other stuff in your dream? The tunnel and the jungle and the voices. Are they real, too?"

After I pass the message, Hook says, "Yeah, she's right. If it's okay with you, George, how about telling it to us in order?"

"Okay. My parents were born in North China, but I wasn't. The ship was full of people from my country. We were running away and —"

"What's the name of your country?" Amie cuts in.

I think hard, but nothing comes. "I don't remember."

"No problem," says Hook. "We know close enough. The computer told us Southeast Asia. There's a few countries in there, but not many."

"I think my father took us onto the ship. But something bad happened so he couldn't come with us." As soon as I say this, I start to feel bad. Until now, I've just been talking, as if all this happened to somebody else. But it didn't. It happened to *me*, and as I remember, I can feel a big hollowness inside and it grows like a black stain.

And the dream feeling comes back. The feeling that something terrible happened and it's my fault.

"I think my younger sister was on the ship," I hear myself saying.

The room is silent except for the low music. Outside, the snow has let up and only light flakes are dancing on the wind. My friends are waiting for me to go on; I can feel it. They don't want to ask me any more, but they want to know more.

"I think the other stuff in the dream, the jungle and the soldiers' bodies in the ditches, comes from before the ship. I don't want to remember that, though."

Heather's hands say, "That's okay, George. Maybe it's better to let it be. You know enough now. And one good thing: maybe your father is okay."

When she says this I begin to feel the tears roll down my cheeks. I feel very bad. I'm sure I have a father but I can't remember anything about him.

Amie gets up and walks slowly into her bedroom. She comes back with a long necklace thing with beads and a silver cross on it. She stands in front of me and feels for my head. I can see my face, all wet now, in her mirrors. She puts the necklace over my head.

"This is called a rosary, George. Maybe it will make you feel better. Today you were sort of reborn, and getting born is painful." Then she feels her way to the swivel chair and sits down. She shuts off the computer.

Hook yawns a big yawn and scratches under his chin with his hook. "I don't know about you guys, but I feel like a game of euchre. Heather, I bet we could whip these two in no time. Absolutely. Whaddya say?"

Heather gets the special Braille cards from the shelf over Amie's desk. We gather around the table and clear some candy and empty Coke cans away to make room.

"And listen you, George Horse, no peeking into Amie's mirrors so you can see what cards she's got!" He smiles.

I laugh. I am laughing and crying at the same time.

Heather starts to deal. After we play I will go home in the snow and talk to Bob and Mitzi. I've got a lot to tell them.

PART
TWO

14

"Hah! I made it," Mitzi says to me. "Crown me, please."

"Okay. But it won't do you any good. I'm going to win anyway."

"Oh, no. Just because you won the last two games out of three, it doesn't mean you'll be lucky again!"

"We'll see," I answer.

"Want another muffin? I'm going to have one."

"Yes, please."

Mitzi goes to the stove and takes two hot muffins out of the baking tin. She drops them on our plates and blows on her fingers, then pours herself another coffee.

Outside the kitchen window a huge clear icicle hangs from the eaves trough. It is lit up like a bulb by the bright sunlight that pours through the window. Water drips from the icicle's point and we can hear it plop onto the driveway.

"I saw a robin today," says Mitzi as she sits down. "Bet

he's the first one of the year. The snow's not quite gone yet.''

I tear the muffin in half and steam comes from inside. I put a blob of butter on one of the halves. It melts into the muffin.

"It's my move," I say, and I jump two of her checkers at once.

"Dirty rat," she says and laughs. She takes a sip of the coffee, then tucks her long red hair behind her ears. Her forehead creases. "Hmmmm. Now what am I going to do? Maybe . . ."

Her hand hangs above one of her checkers. The one I am hoping she'll move.

The phone rings.

"Saved by the bell," she says as she gets up. "All the same, I wish the phone wouldn't work on Sunday afternoons."

After she says Hello she listens for a minute. The smile falls away.

"Oh, no. No," she moans.

I stop chewing and stare at the black phone.

"Okay, I'll tell him," she says and hangs up. "That was Hook, George. Heather's had an accident. She's in the hospital."

Fear hits me like a sharp slap. "What happened? Is she okay?"

"Hook didn't know any details. She wasn't hurt really badly, but that's all he could tell me. He's picking up Amie then coming by to get you. His mother will drive the three of you to the hospital. You'd better get ready."

"That's her room," Hook says, "number 528."

The room is near the end of a long hallway that smells

like medicine and cleaning fluid. I turn the wheelchair and shove it against the door, pushing it open. Amie's hand grips my arm tightly as we go inside and the door hisses shut behind us.

The room is gloomy and dim. The curtains are drawn and a weak glow comes from a small lamp above the single bed. It takes a few seconds before I can see anything.

When I see the figure propped up in the bed I stop.

"No, no. Not that!" I realize it is me talking.

"What's the matter?" Amie says. Her voice is shaking.

Hook answers. "Her head is all bandaged up, Amie, and so are her eyes."

Heather rolls over and faces the window curtains.

"Oh God," Amie cries out. "Her eyes?" She begins to sob.

The three of us stay still, afraid to go to the bed.

"Now hang on," Hook says evenly. "It might not be so bad. Let's not jump to conclusions."

"What should we do, Hook?" I ask.

"We go over there and let her know we're here, that's what. Push, George."

It's hard to push properly because Amie is gripping my arm and hanging back. The chair bumps the bed and Heather's head turns very slowly toward us. Her face is pale below the bandages. Her mouth is a hard, straight line.

Her hands move fast. "Who's there?"

Hook taps her arm with his hook. She closes her hand on the hook and the hard line disappears. She signs again.

"She says are all three of us here? Tap her once for *Yes* and twice for *No*."

Hook taps her once.

Amie feels her way around to the window side of the bed. Gently her fingers check out the bandages on Heather's head. Then they travel down her arm. She holds

Heather's hand. I can see the tears rolling down from under her mirrors. One tear falls and splashes on Heather's hand.

Heather gently takes her hands away and begins to sign. "She says don't cry, Amie. She's okay."

"Tell her that's a relief. I was afraid she was going to be like me."

"I can't tell her. She can't see me."

"Yeah, smarten up, Dum-dum," says Hook. I can hear the relief in his voice. "Besides, to be like you she'd need a dye job."

Amie laughs. She wipes her tears away, pushing her fingers up under her glasses.

"They bandaged my eyes because I got a concussion," Heather's hands say. "They want my eyes to keep still for a couple of days."

Hook is telling me what a concussion is but I am not listening. There is something wrong with her signing, but I don't tell the others. She pauses a lot, as if she isn't sure of herself. But it's more than that.

"Do you want to know what happened?" ask her hands.

When I translate, Hook taps her arm once.

"Well, I was working late in our variety store last night. Mom and Dad were upstairs in our apartment watching TV and my brother was on a date. It was eleven o'clock and I was getting ready to close up. When I went to lock the front door I saw a cop car and a fire engine go past. They weren't going very fast but their lights were flashing like crazy.

"So I went out on the sidewalk to see what was going on. You know how nosey I am." She tries to smile.

"Sure do," Hook agrees. Then he remembers and taps her arm once. Then Amie taps the other arm. Then I squeeze her foot. Heather smiles, for real this time.

"Okay, okay, I get the message. Anyway, the cop car and

fire engine were stopped in the middle of the street, right in front of the Italian restaurant about two blocks away. It was hard to see because of all the lights bouncing off the buildings and the ice on the road, and there were tons of people milling around. I was trying to decide whether to get my coat and join the crowd. Without thinking about it, I stepped off the curb, squeezed between two parked cars, and stood in the street.

"I could see a lot better from there. The firemen turned on some flood lights and I saw smoke boiling out of a window of the apartment above the restaurant. There was a ladder up to the window but nobody was on it yet. Some firemen were running in and out of the doorway. Others were pulling long hoses from the back of the truck. Cops were pushing back the crowd, making a big ring of people in front of the building.

"Another fire truck went past me, followed by an ambulance, both going slowly. And that should have given me the clue. Why were emergency vehicles going *slowly*?"

Heather's hands speeded up. "While I was standing in the street shivering I was breaking the most important rule there is for someone like me: *never* turn your back on *anything* that might be dangerous. You know that hill right by our store? It had a lot of ice on it. *That's* why the cops and the rest of them were taking it easy!"

Heather stops signing and slams her fist — *whack!* — into her palm, once, twice, three times. Her mouth is a thin line again. Her signing turns harsh.

"What an idiot I was! Acting like some fool who'd gone deaf the day before. How could I do something so stupid!"

She pauses for a little before going on. "I guess a car came down the hill and lost control on the ice. All I remember is that the car that was parked beside me suddenly jumped sideways and forward at the same time, as if someone had jerked it with a string, and it squashed into the car in front of it. The metal on both cars bent and folded. Bits of glass and red plastic flew into the air. I remember thinking how weird it looked — just before I felt myself getting hit, then flying, flying through the air. Then nothing.

"I was lucky. The doctor said I've got lots of scrapes and bruises and a concussion, but nothing broken."

The words I translate make it sound as if Heather feels lucky. But her signing when she says that is choppy. Now her hands lie on the blankets and her fists are clenched.

The door hisses open and a nurse walks quickly into the room. She is short and fat and has pimples on her face. She has a tiny paper cup in her hand.

"Excuse me," she says to Hook. "I have to get to the bed."

"Sorry," he mutters, and struggles to work the chair back out of her way.

"And how are we this afternoon? Enjoying your visit with your friends, here?" There is no warmth in the nurse's voice. "Time for your medication."

She takes a glass half full of water from the bedside table. "Would you like to take these, or shall I feed them to you?"

She waits for a few seconds, then says, "Now come, come, dear. Don't be like this. I've many other patients to see. I can't spend all day with you. Take your medicine like a good —"

Heather's hands lift off the blankets. She wants to sign, but her hands knock the glass and the little paper cup flying. The pills hit the nurse in the face.

"What's that?" Amie squeals as the glass bounces off her arm, splashing her, and crashes to the floor.

Heather sucks in her breath. "What's that? Who is it?" ask her hands, just as the nurse says, "*Damn!* Can't you be more careful?''

Hook's voice cuts through, like a punch. "She can't hear you, you stupid idiot. She's *deaf*."

Heather is jerking her head from side to side. Her fists pound on the bed, then fly up like scared birds. "What's *wrong*? Who *is* that? Where's George?" Her fists pound again.

The nurse backs away from the bed, bumping Hook's chair. Her face is red.

"Oh, I'm sorry! I didn't — I'll get more —" She turns and hurries out of the room.

I step quickly to Heather's side. I catch her wrists. She fights me for a second, then I lean down and hold her fists against my eyes. The hands relax and open. She traces her fingers over my face, then pulls me down and hugs me. I can feel the tightness flow away from her.

I straighten up, still holding her hands. I guide the hands to make the sign for *It's okay*.

She takes her hands away. "I'm all right, now. Tell the others I want to be alone now. Come back tomorrow after school, okay?"

I tell the others. Hook works the chair in close and taps Heather's arm once. Amie leans down and kisses her, then feels her way around the bed.

We leave Heather lying there alone, her arms stiff, her fists clenched. Her mouth is a hard line again. We don't want to go but we have to do what she wants.

The door hisses shut behind us.

Amie shuffles along beside me, very slowly. Her arm is on my shoulder. In the elevator she stands quietly with her head down.

Hook stares at her. He keeps looking until the doors slide open.

On the way home in the car he says to his mother, "Mom, how about dropping Amie off and bringing

George back to our place?"

"Sure, dear."

"Okay with you, George?"

"Okay with me, Hook."

I know the look on his face. There's something on his mind.

馬

"Well, that's certainly good news," says Hook's mother as she parks the car. He has been giving her a report on Heather's condition.

Hook's mother is really nice. She is small, but strong, with curly black hair like Hook's.

She locks the car and heads toward the house. I turn Hook's chair to follow but he tells me to take him to the big garage at the end of the driveway.

Inside, the garage is dark. "There's a switch to the right of the doorway, George."

The lights flood the place and I see right away it's a garage only on the outside. Inside, it's a huge room, with bright wallpaper. Carpet covers half the floor. This half of the room looks like a study. There's a sound system, reading lamp, easy chair, and desk. Stacks of magazines and shelves stuffed with manuals.

But the other half is a workshop. The floor is gray-painted cement. A work bench stretches along one wall, wheelchair height, with dozens of tools hanging above it. There's a sink and some machines along the other wall.

In the middle of the floor are two huge motorcycles. One is up on the center stand, like in a showroom. Light sparkles and gleams on the chrome fenders and the chrome trim on the motor. This motorcycle is painted metallic blue and on the teardrop shaped gas tank is the word *Triumph*.

The second motorcycle looks like a skeleton — just an apple-red frame with the motor.

I look down at Hook. He shrugs off his coat and tosses it over to the easy chair. "Well, what do you think? Beautiful, or what?" He is smiling now.

"Yeah, nice, Hook." I take off my parka and throw it on top of his.

"Know what these babies are, George? They're Triumph Bonnevilles. Classics. Haven't been manufactured for years. They go like oiled lightning. You oughta hear the sexy growl those six-fifties make. They're named after a place in the state of Utah where they used to hold speed trials — the Bonneville Salt Flats.

"I bought 'em in crates a long time ago and —"

"In crates?"

"Yeah. I mean, when cycles are shipped from the factories, they aren't assembled. They're packed in pieces into big crates. These have been in storage for years and years. I pulled the engines to bits to make sure all the parts survived the storage, then built them from the floor up. Or at least one of them. Red over there needs a couple of days' more work before she's road ready. But Blue is all set to tear. Absolutely. Push me closer, willya?

"Ever been on a cycle, George?"

"No, of course not. We didn't have *these* in our village, Hook!"

"Nice memory, George Horse. Usually you say, 'I don't think so.' Anyway, take a look. See the calipers on the handlebars? The left one is the clutch — for shifting gears. The right one is the front brake. Got it?"

"Got it."

"Look at Blue. See that little pedal down beside the engine? Footbrake for the back wheel. Over here on the left side is the gear-change lever. You operate it with your foot. This is the horn button, headlight switch — on/off and high-beam —"

I have stopped listening. Because something Hook said has just hit me. He said he built this cycle to travel on. How could he? He'd have to use both feet! I tune in again.

"— see the second set of foot pegs over there on Red? They're for the passenger. Now, look at this cycle."

The blue one doesn't have pegs. It has platforms, just like the ones on Hook's chair, but these are thinner with leather straps on them.

"Now, check out the saddle."

The long seat is covered with soft black leather and has a tall padded backrest with a safety belt attached.

"This frame welded over the rear fender I made myself. I sent it out to be chromed. This will hold my chair once it's folded up. Just hang it here —" he points to two clamps —"and tighten up the wing nuts. Neat, right?"

"But, Hook. I don't get it. How can you drive a motorcycle?"

"Hey, George. You don't *drive* a cycle. You *ride* it. No, I can't ride it. I'm the passenger."

"Then who —"

"Take a guess, pal."

Hook and I are still in his workshop. He's in the easy chair and I'm using the desk chair. On the floor between us is a pizza box, empty. Hook drains his Coke and flips the can into the box.

"Okay, George Horse. Time for old Hook to cut out the mystery, right?"

"Right. What's the plan?"

"Well, originally I bought the cycles for a hobby. You know, something to do at night and on rainy weekends. Figured I'd sell them and make a few bucks. There's always a market for cycles like that. But then I sort of grew attached to old Blue there, and I hatched this crazy scheme about you and me taking a trip this summer. I could teach you to ride within a month. You're sixteen now and you could get a license easily. I could keep Blue, sell Red, and still make a profit."

I don't like this idea too much. I look over at the blue cycle. It is not beautiful to me. It looks ugly and heavy and strong. How could I control it? But Hook is still going.

"But today I changed my mind again. I began to work on a *real* crazy plan."

He scratches his nose with his hook and says in a low voice, "Did you see Amie today? Did you notice?"

I know right away what he means.

"Her confidence went up in smoke, didn't it, George? I mean, she crept along beside us like a sick old lady. Absolutely."

"Maybe she'll get over it, Hook."

"Yeah, maybe. But she fell into a big hole there, George. She lost it. And if she lost it today, she can lose it again."

I sip my Coke, thinking. I remember the way Amie felt in Robinsons' Bush that day. And the way Hook acted after the Black Ones almost killed him. The no-power feeling. Then I tell him about Heather — how her signing showed me that she had lost it, too.

"Yeah, well, it's not surprising. Poor Heather. When I think about it, I get the chills. Imagine what it's like to get whacked by a car like that, and not have *any* idea that it's coming! And she knows it can always happen again.

"So here's my crazy idea. Now, hold still 'til you hear all of it. The *four* of us take a cycle trip! Soon as school gets out in June. We can get to Algonquin Provincial Park in a few hours' ride, easily. I've got some camping gear and I can borrow more from my cousin. And if it works out, we can take more trips. Anywhere we want.

"So you'll have to learn to ride, and you'll have to help me teach Heather. Amie and I are strictly pillion seat, right?"

"Uh, I guess so, Hook."

"The thing is, George Horse, the Cripples' Club needs to pull off a caper like this so that when we get back home, we never need to be afraid of *anything*, ever again."

Hook leans back in his chair. He has that look on his face again, the one he had when we left the hospital.

"Are you with me?" he says quietly.

"I'm with you, Hook."

He holds out his left hand and we shake.

"But how will we convince our parents, Hook?"

"One step at a time," he answers. "First, we have to convince the girls."

15

Today is the first day of a new month — June.

And today is my first "solo."

The sun has been up for about an hour and I can feel its heat as soon as I step out the side door. But I'm dressed up warm. I have two sweaters under my jacket, and a wool scarf wrapped tight under my collar.

Blue is still coated with dew. I take a soft cloth from the saddle bag and wipe the chilly mist off the bright fenders, the tank, and the soft leather saddle. Then I put the cloth away and pull on my helmet. It is metallic blue, with a white running horse on each side above the ear. Hook bought it for me when I got my license last week and painted the horses on himself. I put on my lined leather gloves and tighten the wrist straps. After I insert the key and pull the choke I straddle the cycle, knocking the kickstand up with my foot.

The cycle starts with the first kick and I rev her up

slowly for a minute. The growl of the engine echoes off
the side wall of the house. After I flick on the headlight I
push in the choke and roll down the driveway.

The morning air is cool on my face as I ride through
town. The streets are crowded with cars taking people to
work and I move through the traffic. I pull up at a
stoplight and put my feet down. The cycle is tall and
heavy and I have to stand on the balls of my feet. But I am
not afraid of it any more. It has good balance.

I power smoothly away from the light, leaving the cars
behind, and after a few minutes I am passing under the big
highway. The cars drift by above me, fast and silent. I turn
onto the two-lane highway that goes from our town to the
next. Climbing up through the gears, I am soon doing
sixty and I level off.

The wind is cold at this speed and it presses my jacket
hard against my chest. My face tingles around my goggles
and my nose soon feels like a blob of snow. Icy knives jab
at my neck, poking under the scarf, and cold needles prick
through the thick socks above my work boots. Already my
fingers have stiffened a little on the handgrips.

But the icy stabs are nice. My body is warm and the air
feels fresh and crisp — new. The wind roars inside my
helmet and just under my knees the engine rumbles
smoothly.

A mile or so past the big highway, the two-lane begins
to curve and swoop, making its way over and between the
hills. The fields are brown but the trees at their edges are
fresh green. Soft white ground mist lies in the low spots.
There is a rich new earth smell on the cool air.

The white lines flash away behind me. The road blurs
past, rushing under my feet. I lean into the curves, steering
with my weight. I crank the right handgrip and the
speedometer needle jumps to sixty-five and the engine
grumbles a little louder.

Above and ahead of me I see a hawk floating way up in the clear sky. He is like a sharp pencil point, writing invisible circles on the blue as he rides the wind. Below him, I am gliding inches above the blacktop, drawing an invisible line on the earth. There are no cars ahead and nothing in my mirrors.

I know what Hook means now. Out here I feel free. Just me and the cycle and the road stretching to the horizon. I feel strong. A hot rush begins deep inside me and rises through my chest and into my head. I can feel a smile spread across my face and the icy wind on my teeth. I crank the handgrip a little more. I want to ride and ride.

After a while I check the watch on my left wrist. I am surprised to see I've been out for an hour. I don't want to, but I back off on the gas and begin to kick down through the gears. I pull off onto a gravel side road — carefully, because the cycle wants to slide on the stones. I get off and turn the key.

I take off my helmet and gloves and unzip my jacket. The silence rushes in. But then I hear birds, and the ticks of the engine as it starts to cool. The sun soaks the chill out of me. I lean against the cycle and look out across a valley made of brown squares, green patches, and white lines. Above it the hawk still circles. A car hisses past on the blacktop.

I am starting to believe we can do it.

Maybe Hook's plan for the trip *isn't* so crazy. Heather is going to start to ride Red in a couple of days. She is practicing on the 50cc Honda Hook borrowed from his cousin. She's a good rider. She'll have her license soon, then she can ride out here with me.

What will it be like? I wonder. The idea doesn't scare me now. Not as much, anyway. Not after this morning's ride.

I check my watch. Time to go back. In no time I am roaring back to town.

I am late, so I decide to ride right to school. I will take the cycle home at lunchtime. Hook says we shouldn't leave it in the school parking lot too much. When I turn through the gate into the lot I see classes must have started. There's nobody around.

Except a black van moving slowly down the rows of cars.

I know that van.

I slip the cycle into an empty parking spot, turn it off, dismount, and pull it up onto the center stand. I take the key out and take off my helmet.

The van creeps down the row and stops behind me. I hear the driver's window roll down and I turn to see Silverheels poke his head out. I can see his long hair and the red spots on his face.

"Hey, Rice! What's new?"

I don't answer.

"Where'd ya get the antique wheels, Rice? Comin' up in the world, are ya?"

The van door opens and Silverheels gets out. He leaves the door open and I can hear heavy rock music pounding inside. His boots sound hollow as he walks over to the cycle.

He takes a good look at the cycle, moving around it slowly. I watch him carefully. I unzip my jacket. It's hot.

Silverheels talks without looking at me. "Yeah, nice bike. By the way, Rice, I meant to talk to you about what you did to my three boys last winter."

I take a little step backwards. I'm not sure what he means at first. Then I remember Amie held up against a fence by Black Ones. I say nothing. But I start to get mad.

"Those three guys were out of line," he goes on. He is still looking the cycle over, not raising his eyes. "They deserved what they got." He squats down to look at the engine closely. He is on the other side of the cycle and all I see is the top of his head. "Problem is, Rice . . . now I gotta do something about that. Can't let it get around that a short-ass like you can hold us down. I would have taken care of it before but I've been . . . away."

He laughs. He straightens up, wiping his hands on his black T-shirt. "Sort of a holiday." He jams his hands in the back pockets of his jeans. He's looking at me now.

"Anyway, like I said, we got a score to settle. Know what I mean?"

I'm not sure what he means at all, so I don't answer. We stand, looking at each other. The sun beats down on us. The rock music pounds away.

I turn and walk toward the school, expecting to hear boot heels following me. But all I hear is the music.

It's the day after, and Hook and I are sitting in chairs on his front lawn, watching Heather. She is practicing on the Honda, turning in and out of the driveway. Each time she passes, she waves. The Honda's little engine sounds like an angry bee and the sunlight flashes in the mirrors.

"Wonder what the ol' scumbag's up to now?" Hook says, staring up through the new buds on the big tree at the roadside.

"What? Oh. I don't know, Hook."

"I mean, it's funny that he warned you. If he wanted revenge, he and his goons would have just jumped you. He's not going to come after Heather or Amie or me, I don't think. From what he told you, we know he thinks it's off limits to come after us. So maybe he's gonna come after you, George."

Heather jumps the curb and heads the Honda straight for Hook's chair. He laughs and pretends to be scared to death, throwing his arms up to cover his face. The Honda putt-putts between our chairs, wobbling on the soft grass. Heather has a big grin on her face. Her blue eyes sparkle.

"Tell her to practice emergency stops, George."

I walk over to the driveway and wait 'til Heather comes by again. When I tell her what Hook said she signs Okay and turns out onto the street. With a piece of white chalk I draw a line on the road in front of our chairs.

When I drop into my chair Hook talks. "I want you to be careful, okay?"

Hook's warning makes me nervous. "Okay, Hook."

We hear an angry buzz and Heather comes tearing down the road, doing about forty, and pulls the Honda up short. Her front wheel crosses the white chalk line I drew on the road. She looks over at Hook. His head shakes. She turns the little cycle and drones off down the street again.

"Does anybody know what he's been up to?" I ask.

"Yeah. The cops told my uncle that he's still pushing. He was caught and sent to jail for a few months, but he's out again. I guess us helping him to graduate — even if he didn't want to — didn't cut down his action any. Now he's got more time to get down to business. I don't think Siggy accomplished much after all."

This time Heather stops right on the line. Hook makes the Okay sign that I taught him and Heather asks, "Again?"

I nod. Hook nods. Off she goes again.

"Well, let's not let Silverheels ruin our day, George. If he's got something in mind, we'll know soon enough. Let's roll Red out of the shop. I think our redhead is ready. Hey, red on Red! Classic, right? Absolutely!"

16

"How can you do that?" Bob wonders. "Doesn't it hurt your legs?"

I look up at him, squinting into the glare of the morning sun behind him. He is wearing shorts and a T-shirt, but sweat shines on his brow and shows wet spots on his shirt. He leans on the old lawnmower.

"How can I do what, Bob?"

"Squat like that. And work at the same time."

I am in the middle of the flowerbed, tearing out weeds. Damp black dirt squishes between my toes. My hands and bare legs are dirty. The earth has a strong, damp smell. The odor of the flowers is light and sweet.

I don't know what Bob means. I am squatting in the garden, bent over, knees pointing straight up. I stretch between my knees to get at the weeds. I can feel the sun on my back and shoulders, dirt under my fingernails, sweat on my body. I am never afraid here.

"If I managed to squash myself into that position," Bob goes on, "which I doubt I could, I'd never get up again. *And* I'd ache for a week. I think you're made of rubber, George."

It's a joke. I can tell from the tone of his voice. I laugh and keep tearing up weeds. Bob turns the lawnmower around and pushes it clattering into the little metal shed in our little yard. The wet grass clippings stick to the wheels of the mower and the bottoms of his running shoes.

He comes back with a hoe. It doesn't look right to me. I don't know why. He starts to work on the part I've weeded, scraping the loose dirt between the red and white flowers. He breaks up the lumps with little chops of the hoe.

You aren't supposed to use a hoe like that. It should have a longer handle and a wider blade. You raise it high above your head and bring it down hard and fast into the wet yellow clay — *thunk* — then pull back hard on the long handle, turning the wedge of yellow clay over. Later the water buffalo drags the plow back and forth, breaking up the wedges and —

"Mitzi says these flowers are the best we've ever had back here, ol' buddy. You've got a green thumb."

Bob's voice comes from behind me as I move slowly through the flower garden that borders the small green patch of lawn. I toss the weeds onto the grass as I go.

I look at my thumb. It's black from the dirt.

"Hey, you know what month this is?"

"Sure, Bob." I keep working. "June. The . . . fourteenth."

"Right. Betcha can't tell me the other months. In order."

The scrape of the hoe in the dirt fills the spaces between the words as I slowly tell him the months.

"Well, well. Not bad. Now, how about —"

"George!" Mitzi's voice from the window at the back of the house. "Hook just phoned. I said you'd call back when you're finished. He sounds upset about something."

"Bad news, George Horse." Hook's voice on the phone is serious, edged with anger. "Blue is missing."

"What happened, Hook?"

"I had both cycles parked behind the house," he rushes on. "Right where you left Blue the day before yesterday. And when I came outside this morning it was gone! Whoever ripped it off left the tarp behind. The helmets are gone, too."

I sink slowly into a kitchen chair.

"What should we do, Hook?"

"I got a good idea who ripped it off, don't you?"

"No, Hook, I —"

"Silverheels," he hissed. "I'd lay money on it."

I say nothing, listening to him breathing at the end of the line.

"How about we pay him a visit, George. I looked up his address in the phone book. We can get there by bus."

"It would be easy for him to do it." Hook is thinking out loud as I roll him along his street to the bus stop. The rubber wheels clunk over each crack between the cement squares of the sidewalk, making his legs shake.

The neighborhood is full of Saturday sounds: droning lawnmowers, snipping hedge shears, hissing hoses. A kid flashes past on a skateboard.

I don't like the idea of going to Silverheels's place. What if the Black Ones are there?

"He could have parked his van down the street from my house," Hook goes on. "In the middle of the night sometime. He could have rolled the cycle out the driveway, down the street, and up a plank into the van. Two or three minutes is all it would have taken."

"Are you sure it was him, Hook?"

We are at the bus stop, now. I can see the bus down the street. The sun flashes in the windshield.

"Pretty sure."

The old blue and white bus squeals to a stop. The engine growls. The doors flap open — *psssss*. How will Hook get on? I wonder. We have never done this before.

"Turn me sideways to the door, George. Close. No, the other way, facing the front. Now, help me up onto the bottom step."

Hook puts his left hand flat on the step and I grab him by his hook arm and swing him up onto the step. When I look up I see the driver has gotten out of his seat. Without even thinking, I shake my head. He sits down again.

Hook lifts himself backwards up the two steps to the aisle. His muscles flex under his T-shirt. He grabs his stick legs under the knees and swings them up, then levers himself backwards down the aisle a few feet to an empty seat. Then he reaches above his shoulder, laying his forearm on the seat. I bend, brace him under his other arm and help lift him up onto the seat. The other people on the bus stare, but pretend not to.

While he slides over to the window I go back out the door and fold up his chair. I carry it onto the bus. The door slaps shut behind me — *pssss* — and the bus begins to rumble forward.

I steady myself and reach into the pocket of my shorts. "How much?" I ask the driver.

"Forget it," he says, without looking at me.

I make my way back to the seat and sit down. I prop the

metal tube chair in the aisle.

"Not everybody," says Hook to the window, "gets the ass of his jeans dirty getting on a bus."

Silverheels's neighborhood is on the edge of town. There are no sidewalks on his street so I have to push Hook along the edge of the bumpy black pavement. There are lots of potholes in the road. Ditches with scummy water in them run down each side. The ditches make me nervous.

The houses on this street are small, old, and tired. They have gravel driveways and lawns that slope to the ditches.

We have been on the street for about fifteen minutes when Hook says, "Stop." He squints at a house on the left. "Yep. Number 369. That's it."

Silverheels's house is farther back off the road than the others. It is small, made of red brick. There are shingles missing from the roof and paint peels from the wood trim. There is a cement porch at the front door. A woman is sitting in a rocking chair, facing down the street. She is wearing slippers and a wrinkled green dress. Her sweater is buttoned up crooked. Her gray hair is held in a pony tail with an elastic band.

The woman is holding a can of beer in one hand and a cigaret in the other. She takes a long pull on the cigaret and smoke rolls out of her nose. She balances the beer on the chair arm, then pulls a crushed cigaret pack from the sweater pocket. She lights a new cigaret on the butt of the old one. The butt sails off the porch, smoking. She stuffs the pack away and picks up the beer can.

"Little early to soak up the suds," Hook mumbles.

The woman has not noticed us yet. What will Hook do? I wonder. I push him along in front of the house.

A phone rings from inside. The woman tips the beer

can up, tilting her head back. She heaves herself out of the rocker. She is not very tall, but she is very round. She walks carefully into the house, letting the metal screen door bang behind her.

Beside Silverheels's house is a long dirt driveway leading to an old wooden garage.

"If he ripped off the cycle," says Hook, pointing, "it'll be in there. Let's go, before she comes out again."

The driveway is rutted and bumpy. It's hard to push the chair. I don't like this idea too much.

I take a look at the front door, but the woman does not appear. We roll, bumping, past the porch. There is a side door, too, but it's closed. When I get Hook to the garage he says, "Take a peek, George."

The wide doors are the kind that swing open to the side. There's a row of small, dirty windows on each door but they are too high for me to look into. There is a wide space where the doors join. It's dark inside and I can't see much.

But the light leaking through the windows glints on chrome. Blue is in there, up on its center stand.

"Well?" Hook's voice makes me jump.

"It's in there, Hook, I can see it."

What should we do now? I wonder. The woman will catch us if we try to take the cycle. I look back at the side door. It's still closed.

"Swing the door open and let's mount up," says Hook. His voice has a hard edge. "I brought the key."

I do as he says. The door creaks and groans as I pull it open. Will the woman hear us? The garage smells damp inside. There's a bench on the back wall with junk piled all over it. Beside the cycle an old car sits up on blocks. The hood, trunk, and doors are open. It looks like a dead insect.

There is a wooden box beside the cycle with a lot of tools on it.

"Looks like our friend the thief was all set to strip her down," Hook says. "Is there any damage, George?"

I step over to the cycle and nervously look it over. Our helmets still hang from the hooks under the seat. "It looks okay," I tell him, turning to face him as I talk. "Hook, do you really think —"

A black van turns into the driveway.

The engine of the van roars as it races up the driveway in a cloud of dust. It skids to a stop, inches from Hook's chair.

17

The door of the van flies open. Silverheels's black cowboy boots and blue-jean legs appear below it as he jumps out. The door slams. He walks slowly toward us. Even though it's hot now he is wearing a black leather jacket over his blue T-shirt.

Silverheels tosses his cigaret onto the ground. "What the hell are you doing here, half-man?" he sneers. Then he catches sight of me in the garage. "Brought Rice-brain with you, eh?"

"Just stand out of the way and let us pass," Hook says, his voice even. "Any trouble and we go to the cops."

Silverheels grins and runs his fingers through his long hair. His eyes flick to the house, then back.

I'm trapped in the garage. How can I get the cycle out? How can Hook and I get away? We're trapped in the space between the van and the garage.

"Ah hell, you might as well take that pile of nuts and

bolts," Silverheels says. "Probably couldn't have gotten much for it anyway. But before you leave, I got a score to settle with the chink." He stretches his arm toward me, then crooks his fingers. "Come on out, Rice."

His eyes flick to the side door of the house again. He takes off his jacket and hangs it on the handle of Hook's chair. Hook reaches back and shoves it off. It drops onto the dirt of the driveway.

"Leave George out of this," Hook says. "You touch him and we go to the cops for sure. Let us go, and we'll forget your latest rip-off."

"I got no worries about cops, half-man."

Hook's voice is hard. "Look, you jerk —"

Silverheels quickly grabs the handles of Hook's chair, spins him around, and runs him up against the grille of the van. The bang knocks Hook forward and I can hear his body whack against the van.

I step out of the garage into the sunlight. I can feel the anger rise inside me. Hot, like a wave. I fight to keep my breathing even. Silverheels turns and faces me. He has a roll of fat around his middle but his shoulders and arms are thick.

"We don't seem to get along too well, do we Rice? Might as well get things settled."

While he's talking, I kick off my shoes and peel off my socks. Breathing evenly, I wait. With a last quick look at the door of the house he steps toward me. His arms are up, like a boxer on TV. His body is bent a little at the waist.

He starts to circle. He moves in fast, jabbing at my head. I step back out of the way. He swings again. Misses. I do not strike back. There is lots of time. He moves in again, swinging — *one, two*. I duck the first, block the second, step to the side.

"Come on. Fight, coward!" he hisses. He comes in again with the same *one, two*. This time the second catches me on the shoulder, knocks me back a bit. But I get my balance in time to side-step his kick. He's starting to breathe hard.

I have the feel of the ground under my bare feet now. I know his moves. *"Gùo lái,"* a low voice says. It is my voice. *Come on.* He moves in, *one, two.* Misses. He's off balance a little. I hook a punch into his left ear. When it lands, it sounds like a slap. Silverheels yelps with the pain. I step back and wait.

He's mad now. His face reddens. He hawks and spits, crouches a bit more. He fakes a kick and comes in after the fake with a punch to my stomach. I side-step, blocking the punch down and to the side. He is off balance. His ribcage is open. I punch him there twice, *whack, whack!*, and slide back again. Half his chest has no more air in it. He straightens slowly, trying to get his breath back. Turns to face me. Quickly I step to the side again, plant my right foot and roundhouse kick him on the forehead. I curl my toes under and get him with the top of my foot so I don't break the bone. The kick lands solidly — *whap!* — and he falls backwards.

Hook has been watching, his body twisted around so he can see. "Hey, *all right*, George Horse!" he yells.

Silverheels hauls himself to his feet. He jams a hand into his jeans, pulls it out again. *Click!* The sun flashes on a blade in his hand.

"Hey, now wait a second!" Hook's voice comes from behind me. I can hear Silverheels panting. There is a red patch on his forehead. But all my concentration is on the knife. It floats in the air as he tosses it from hand to hand. He crouches again, still tossing the knife. He grins.

Snap! My kick catches the knife in midair and it spins up and over Silverheels's head. I hardly notice the sting in my foot. Silverheels starts to edge back so he can pick up the knife.

"Kevin!" a woman's voice shrieks. A door slams open.

Silverheels makes a mistake. He turns toward the voice, a look of surprise on his face. He darts a look back at me. Then to the woman. He drops his hands and straightens up.

"What are you *doing*?" the woman whines. She is standing outside the door, one hand on the red brick. In the other is a beer can. She stands there swaying for a few seconds, then walks slowly toward us, stepping carefully. "You're in trouble again, aren't you?"

Hook talks over his shoulder. "He stole my cycle, ma'am. It's in the garage. We just came to get it back."

Her face is puffy and white. Her sweater is still buttoned up crooked. She looks at Hook in his chair shoved up against the van. Then at Silverheels. "God *damn* you!" she shrieks. "Not again!" With a clumsy movement she fires the beer can. It spins through the air, slopping foam, and hits Silverheels on the chest. Beer splashes on his shirt, up onto his face. The can falls to his feet.

His eyes dart to me, back to the woman, back to me again. He's trying to decide something. Beer drips from his chin. His shoulders seem to slouch as all the anger drains from his face. He looks embarrassed.

He says nothing. Just turns and walks to the woman. He puts one hand against her back and pushes her toward the house. As they disappear, we can hear her crying and Silverheels's sharp words. "How many times do I have to tell you to stay out of my business!"

In a few minutes the cycle is out by the road and Hook is mounted up. His chair is folded and clamped to the rack. I swing my leg over the seat. Put the key in and turn it. Just before I kick the starter I hear Hook's voice.

"The poor beggar," he says.

We take off down the road, weaving between the potholes. Who does he mean? I wonder. Kevin or his mother?

18

"I'm still not sure about all this," Bob says as he steers our old Chev out of the driveway.

All through breakfast he was quiet and there was a deep line across his forehead. He didn't finish his bacon and eggs. I don't think I've ever seen that happen before.

Mitzi is beside him in the front seat and I'm in the back. The car is pointed into the bright Monday morning sun. Mitzi puts her hand up to cover her eyes.

"Oh, everything will be all right, Bob," she says quietly. "You worry too much."

I can see his eyes in the rearview mirror. He is looking at me. Bob didn't want to let me go on the camping trip. Mitzi talked him into it.

He drives in silence for a while, turning up and down streets, heading to Hook's place. I look out the car window. The neighborhood is waking up. House doors open and newspapers disappear into them.

"Well," Bob says at last, "as long as he keeps his shoes on."

I check the mirror. He is smiling.

At Hook's place we pull my stuff out of the trunk and drop it onto the sidewalk. Bob hugs me. I can feel worry in his squeeze.

"Take it slow and easy, George," he says softly. "Slow and easy, okay?"

"Okay, Bob. I will."

Mitzi hugs me, too, and kisses me on the cheek.

"Remember to phone whenever you can. Every day or so. Call collect. You remember how?"

"I remember. I'll be okay," I add. "Don't worry."

The two of them get back into the old car. Doors slam and the engine wakes. The car moves away. There is an arm sticking out each side — white on one side, black on the other — waving.

I wave back.

I walk around to the back of Hook's place. Before I see them I hear their voices.

"First-aid kit?"

"Check," says Amie.

The two cycles stand in the driveway, pointed toward the road. They don't look sleek and fast anymore. They are like over-fed insects, all bulges and bumps, loaded down with gear.

"Okay, Blue's turn," says Hook. "Tool kit? Hi, George."

Amie turns away from the red cycle and walks carefully to Blue. She feels her way among the lumps as Hook reads from the long list in his hand. The hot morning sun flashes in her mirrors as she bends and straightens.

"Check. Hi, George."

They keep up the chatter as I tie my sleeping bag onto the fork post, just under the headlight, using elastic cords.

Hook's clothes pack is tied to the sissy bar and I transfer my stuff into it from a plastic bag.

"Okay, all set!" Hook shouts.

The screen door slaps shut and Heather comes out followed by Hook's mother, who is drying her hands on her apron. Her mouth is smiling but her eyes aren't.

"Ready to go?" she asks.

"Yep," Hook answers.

His mother leans down and kisses him.

"Well, goodbye then." She waves to us, calls each of our names, then hurries into the house. The door slaps again.

Hook lowers himself out of his chair to the sidewalk. I fold up the chair and hang it on the chrome rack. Soon Amie and Hook are mounted and pulling on their helmets. Amie's is bright silver. Across the back it says NO SYNTAX ERROR. Hook's is blue, to match the cycle, and has a white sock with blue trim painted over each ear.

Heather mounts up, kicks Red to life, and shoves on the bars to get the cycle off the center stand. Her bright yellow helmet is plastered with different colored flowers.

I swing my leg over Blue's saddle and kick the starter. As I rev the engine I see Hook's mother in the kitchen window, watching.

Hook slaps my shoulder. "Come on, Horse. Let's get a move on before everybody drowns in tears."

I guess he saw her, too.

The roads in town are busy, with car jams at all the lights. The cycles are bulky and heavy with all the gear, so the balance is off a bit. That makes it tricky stopping, waiting, and starting off again. Around us, cars cut in and out. Red brake lights flash. Amber directional signals blink. We ride slowly and carefully, stared at by other drivers as they flash past, hurrying to the next stoplight.

Soon we are out on the big three-lane highway. We are drifting along at sixty miles per hour in the center. Heather and I ride side by side so we fill up the lane. Hook says this way is safest, so nobody tries to pass you in your own lane. Each move Heather and I make — changing lanes, passing — we do it smoothly, together.

"You have to ride like you're joined at the hip with a five-foot steel bar," Hook told us again and again. We have practiced this for hours and miles.

I look over at Heather. She sees I am looking and smiles, giving me a thumbs up with her left hand. She loves this. Her bright red hair pokes out from under the flowered yellow helmet and flips in the wind. Her freckles almost dance, she is so happy.

Amie is leaning back on the padded sissy bar. The thin black wires of her Walkman earphones hang from under her helmet. She is slapping her thigh and bobbing her head.

I can feel something move in the small of my back. That means Hook has turned a page.

The highway makes a long curve around our town, then heads north. Soon, it splits. The left part goes straight and the right splits off, then climbs a bridge that curves back over the main highway and disappears behind some hills. Hook's hand appears beside my face, pointing straight. I nod and beep my horn. Amie gets the signal and slaps Heather on the shoulder. Heather looks over and gets the signal from Hook, then nods.

It's a nice day to ride. The sun is up high enough to be warm and there is no wind. The traffic on the highway is light — only a few cars. Once in a while there is a big truck roaring along in the curb lane with a tail of black smoke trailing from the pipe behind the cab. I can hear the tires whining over the rumble of Blue's engine.

The highway is down to two lanes now. There's a low white cement wall between us and the lanes going the other way. Signs on the right talk about good coffee, fresh bait, hamburgers, and how to get to places. Sometimes a bug whacks against my face screen. Our shadows race along beside us, bent into a funny shape.

As the hours pass, the shadows slowly move until they're below the cycles. It's pretty warm, now. I hear a beep and look over at Heather. She points to a sign that says there's a restaurant off the highway a little. I nod and we cut our speed, smoothly pulling off the highway, slowing as we curve along the exit ramp. We kick down through the gears when we see the restaurant and park the cycles in the lot, right by the front doors.

Betty's Grill is small and hot inside. There are lots of guys in check shirts and work boots and baseball caps sitting at the square tables. They give us a long look as I shove Hook's chair between the tables to the back where there's one table left. As she weaves along behind Heather, Amie bumps a fat guy in a denim shirt, jiggling the coffee cup he has in his hand.

She stops and turns her mirrors in his direction. "I'm sorry."

He's looking into his lap, wiping his faded green work pants with a napkin. "Well, Honey, maybe you should watch where you're go —"

As he says this he looks up. Her mirrors are pointed past and above him. His eyes move to Heather, then back to Amie.

"Matter of fact," he corrects himself, "I had my elbow stuck out in your way. My fault, not yours."

"Well, I'm sorry anyway."

"If youse are lookin' for a good lunch," he says, "*don't* order hamburgers. They make 'em outa wood around here. A piece of free advice."

"Thanks," Amie laughs as she moves off again, following Heather.

Everybody is hungry. We order four milks, a big plate of chips to share, and a slab of pizza for each. When the food comes, Hook starts showing off, picking up single chips with his hook without leaving a mark on them.

The restaurant is smoky, full of conversation, the clatter of plates, the clink of spoons and forks. The door opens and closes, tinkling a little bell as customers come and go.

When the food is gone we sit back, letting the ache from the ride creep out of our bones. Heather's hands are flying and I'm busy passing on her favorite school story. One day her English teacher, a short fat guy, was writing on the board and the kids were talking and fooling around while he wasn't looking. He spun around and shouted at them, telling them they had horrible manners and should copy quietly. He turned and started writing again. Then he farted.

The kids laughed like crazy. They could see him stop writing and hunch his shoulders. The back of his neck started to turn red. He was too embarrassed to turn around, but he apologized, still facing the board. He started to write again. After a few seconds, somebody at the back of the room let go with a long, loud raspberry.

The teacher spun around. "Who *did* that?" he screamed. He was so mad that spit flew when he shouted.

After that, every time he turned his back on them, somebody would rip off another raspberry. He was writing Shakespeare stuff and he was so rattled that, instead of writing "Lady Macbeth said, 'But screw your courage to the sticking place,'" he put down, "stick your courage to the screwing place"!

We are all killing ourselves laughing. Heather's head is thrown back and her own brand of laugh, *hiss, hiss, hiss,* mixes with ours. The waitress gives us a dirty look.

"Hey, wait a sec," Hook cuts in. "How did *you* know he farted?"

His question gets Amie going again, giggling like crazy.

"The kid beside me mouthed to me what was happening," Heather's hands answer. "And the first time the teacher twirled around with his face like a red light bulb I *knew* what was going on. It was a panic!"

We are on the road again after lunch, doing about sixty. Hook is reading behind me. Amie is bopping along, slapping her thigh, listening to the Walkman.

The highway curves past farms and hills with lots of trees and sometimes cuts through high gray rock. Sometimes we pass a lake or cross a creek. Wherever there's a lake there are gas stations, restaurants, and lots of signs. Then they drop behind us and we see hills and trees again.

After a while we run into big orange signs telling us there's construction ahead. The speed limit goes down to forty-five, then drops to twenty-five. The cars and trucks on the highway with us start to bunch up and ahead of us brake lights flash and cars dart from one lane to another. In my mirrors all I can see is the front of a big tractor-trailer.

There are all kinds of trucks and earth-moving machines in the distance crawling in and out of a huge cloud of white dust. After another half mile I see what's going on. There's a new bridge stretching across the highway. The space below it is filled with a skeleton of thousands of criss-crossed boards and cement pillars. Yellow dump trucks and earthmovers are crawling around on each side of the bridge, making ramps where the crossroad will climb up to the bridge. White dust hangs over everything and little clouds follow the trucks.

The highway squeezes down to one narrow lane. We have to slow down to walking speed and the cycles are very close together. Hook motions to Heather to go ahead of us. The traffic creeps and stops, creeps and stops.

The sun beats down and the pavement under me is hot. The dust makes my mouth dry. Noise floats in the air with the dust — the growl and roar of the trucks and earth-movers, car engines, the squeal of brakes. Behind me the big tractor-trailer snorts and hisses.

The tractor-trailer and the noise and the cars packed around us make me nervous. I feel trapped.

A big sign says DETOUR and we crawl off the pavement onto a new gravel road. The cycle is hard to control. When I go slowly it wants to wobble. The tires dig into the stones, making it hard to steer. When I get a chance to speed up a bit the rear wheel slides around. Heather is having trouble, too, and Amie is clutching the hold bars on her seat.

We reach the new bridge. A guy up ahead with an orange day-glow vest and yellow hard hat is directing traffic. When a truck rumbles down off the ramp he stops the traffic so the truck can pass. Just as Heather comes up near him he spins the sign he is holding so it reads STOP. When the cycle stops I put my feet out to balance it. My shoes sink into the gravel and it's hard to hold the cycle steady.

Sweat trickles into my eyes, stinging. I feel like I'm cooking. I wish we could get past the noise and dust and get out of here.

I can tell Amie is scared by the swaying cycle because she is clutching Heather's shoulders. That makes it harder for Heather to keep balance.

The guy spins the sign to say CAUTION and waves us ahead. Heather's cycle wobbles forward and crosses the truck path. I have to gun the engine to get our cycle to dig in and pull forward. We creep down a little grade and Heather shoots ahead. Gravel spurts from her back wheel.

Suddenly her handlebars jerk sideways and Heather's body snaps forward over them as if she was yanked by a rope. The cycle crashes to the gravel pitching Amie forward, right over Heather's shoulders. Amie hits the gravel, arms held stiffly in front of her. She rolls a few times and lies still on her stomach about ten feet from the crash. The engine howls. The throttle grip must be jammed into the gravel, holding it open. The back wheel spins like crazy and the chain is a blur.

I jam on my brakes, hard. Hook's body slams into my back and his helmet whacks against mine. Behind me I hear a loud grinding sound, then *psss! psss! psss!* from the tractor-trailer.

Heather rolls slowly onto her back. One foot is caught under the cycle. Amie still isn't moving.

Behind us, car horns start blowing. I am frantic. I dismount, struggling to hold on to the heavy cycle. I pull and yank, trying to wrestle it up onto the center stand, but the stand won't hold in the gravel. I want to drop the cycle — just let it crash down — and run to the girls, but I can't. Hook is strapped on.

"Hey!" Hook is yelling. "Help them! Help them!"

How can I?

I look over my shoulder. He is looking back, too. It's not me he's yelling at. It's the sign man.

I turn back to look at Heather and Amie. Amie pushes herself to her knees, then to her feet. She stands unsteadily, then, holding her arms in front of her, she screams something — two words — and begins to walk. She feels ahead with each foot before she puts it down, and waves her arms back and forth, like someone walking through a room in the dark.

She is walking straight for the cycle.

If she trips over Heather or the cycle, she'll fall and the cycle wheel and chain will tear her to pieces.

"Amie, stop!" Hook shouts from behind me. His voice is panicky. She keeps walking, feeling her way. She doesn't hear Hook. The noise around her — blaring horns, rumbling earth movers, the howling cycle engine — is too much.

Hook shouts in my ear, "Get us over there, George!"

But I can't move. I am frozen. My eyes are locked on Amie.

She is one step away from the cycle now. She feels ahead with her foot and takes a step. The spinning wheel is brushing the cuff of her jeans. She stops. Her arms stick out above the cycle. Below her, the chain is a wicked blur between the engine and the sharp teeth of the wheel sprocket.

"Amie!" Hook screams. "George, *move!*"

The sign man reaches Amie.

He grabs her by the arm and says something to her. She takes a couple of steps backwards and stands still.

Heather struggles to a sitting position. The sign man says something to her, too, then reaches down and shuts off the cycle. The roar dies. He grabs the handle bars of the cycle and heaves. Heather pulls her foot free and gets slowly to her feet. She bends to help him.

I get back on the blue cycle and gun it to life. By the time I get there they have Red back on its wheels. Heather takes Amie's hand and leads her off to the side of the road.

"Get your bike off the road," the sign man says as he begins to shove the red cycle to the side. He has thick tanned arms and the muscles bulge as he pushes.

Behind me I hear the tractor-trailer growl as it begins to move. My hands are shaking so much I can hardly operate the cycle as I kick it into gear, twist the throttle grip, and let the clutch in to move Hook and me over to where the two girls are standing.

Heather has a dirty smear on her cheek where she hit the ground. She is whacking at her legs to get the dust out of her jeans. Amie's arms are scratched up and there's a trickle of blood from her right elbow to her wrist. Her mirror glasses are still on, but they're bent a bit.

"Heather, Amie. You okay?" Hook asks.

"Yeah, I'm all right," Amie answers. Her voice is shaking.

Heather makes the okay sign but her eyes say something else.

"Thanks, man," Hook says to the sign man.

"No problem." He's about twenty-five, a tall, well-built guy, coated with dust. Sweat shines on his forehead. "Listen, if you folks want, you can come over to the trailer to rest for a minute. We got a first-aid kit in there. Or, there's a picnic spot about a half mile up the highway."

"Let's go there," Hook says.

I can see that Heather doesn't really want to get back on the cycle, but she nods. Amie says nothing.

The sign man stops the traffic for us and we pull carefully onto the gravel road. After a few minutes we're off the detour and on paved road again. The road widens to two lanes and the traffic speeds up. The construction noise falls away behind us. We ride side by side, below the speed limit.

We are sitting at a picnic table in the shade of a big tree, sipping Cokes. Amie and Heather have wet hair from washing at the water tap. Heather has changed her T-shirt — the other one got ripped on the cycle mirror when she went over the bars — and Amie has a small bandage on her elbow.

"How's the ankle?" Hook says.

"Okay. It doesn't hurt." Her signing is a little choppy, like that time in the hospital, but not as bad.

Amie's scratched-up hand shakes a bit as she puts her Coke can on the table top. There are lots of names carved in the wood, white scars on the dark stain.

"Maybe this trip wasn't such a good idea," she says in a low voice. "I feel like going home."

I snap a look at Hook. Then at Heather.

"Yeah," her hands agree. "I've had better days." I pass it on.

"Come on guys," Hook says quietly. "Don't let a little thing like this get you down. Don't —"

Whap! Heather's hands slapping together cut him off.

"She says it *wasn't* a little thing," I translate. "They almost got killed."

"Okay, okay, bad choice of words. It was scary as hell. But —"

Amie's mirrors flash. "You don't know what it was like, Hook. It was . . ." Then she stops. Takes a big breath and lets it out slowly. "Sorry. That was a stupid thing to say."

Hook doesn't say anything.

Amie goes on. "But did it ever occur to you that there are *some* things we *can't* do?" Her voice isn't angry — it's tired-sounding.

Heather nods but her hands stay still.

After a few minutes, Hook says, "Yeah, well, maybe. But this isn't one of them. Look how far we've come so far."

I know he isn't talking about miles. Heather and Amie know that, too.

"What's the big deal about camping, anyway?" Amie asks. "We don't even know how to cook."

Heather's hands start to talk, but quit before I can get anything. She takes a sip from her Coke instead.

"So, we'll eat out," Hook jokes.

"Yeah, sure, I suppose there's a McDonald's out in the middle of the bush," Amie says.

"No, there isn't," he admits. "You're right. No McDonald's." Then he leans closer to Amie. Suddenly he jams his hand under her arm and begins to tickle her. She shrieks and starts to giggle.

"It's a Burger King!" he shouts.

"*Hiss, hiss, hiss,*" from Heather as Amie squeals, "Hook, you goof! Cut it out!"

Hook sits up straight and takes a long look at his watch. "Well, we better hit the road if we're gonna get there before dark."

As we pull on our helmets, Amie mumbles, "We ought to have our heads examined."

19

After we've been out on the highway again for a few miles we turn east on Highway 60. It's a two-lane that curves north of a small town then swings south for a few miles before it goes east again. After a while the road begins to loop and dive, passing small lakes and ponds with lots of skinny dead trees in them. The forest presses right to the edge of the road. It's like riding through a crooked green tunnel.

Ahead is a big open area with a stone wall that makes a wide gate. There's a log building there with a flagpole beside it. The flag hangs limp in the heat. We kick down through the gears. A wooden sign set into the stone wall has a yellow animal on it and the words ALGONQUIN PROVINCIAL PARK.

We are close to the log building and I can see that the road splits on either side of it. A tall man with a cup in his hand steps out of the building and waves us past. We don't have to stop.

The two-lane seems to cut right into the trees and disappear up ahead. I am wondering why that building with the wall and the flag were there. I am thinking a lot now.

Because I don't like it here.

The forest seems to press in on us, closing up behind as we move deeper into the trees. Swallowing us. Our shadows race ahead, trying to join the dark shadows in the forest, pulling us toward the dark.

The ponds with the gray tree skeletons scare me. Death all around. Why did Hook think this would be fun?

We pass other signs: CANOE LAKE OUTFITTERS, 100 YDS, PREVENT FOREST FIRES!, SMOKE LAKE CAMP-GROUNDS, 100 YDS. But still no signal from Hook to leave this highway. A few cars pass, going the other way. No one is going in our direction. No one but us.

Finally Hook slaps my shoulder and his hand beside my face points to a sign. REMOTE LAKE CAMPGROUNDS, LEFT, 100 YDS. I beep and Heather drops behind me. We pull off the two-lane onto a narrow bumpy road that disappears into the forest. The trees close in. We head deeper, slower now.

The road opens into a clearing. There's a little log building there. CAMP OFFICE. OBTAIN PERMITS HERE. Beyond it I can see open water, bright in the afternoon sun.

Hook stays on the cycle as the three of us dismount and go inside. Behind a counter stands a tall, skinny old guy with a long face and blond hair. He is wearing a light brown uniform.

"G'day," he calls out. "Come in to register?"

Heather and I fill out the forms and Amie pulls some money out of her jeans. The guy gives us a good looking over. After we pay he pushes some pamphlets across the counter top. Then he writes a big number 56 on our forms and gives us a copy.

"Site number 56, down by the beach," he says. "Nicest site in the campground. No other campers here right now. Not too busy this early in the season. How long you gonna stay?"

"About a week," Amie says.

"Well," he gives us a big smile, "hope you get good weather. Anything you need, just come up here and see me. I'm here 'til six every night."

Our campsite is very private. On one side a huge rock, as tall as Amie, bulges out of the dark ground. It is streaked with dry gray moss. On the other side is a wall of dark evergreens, like Christmas trees. The flat ground between is covered with leaves and pine needles. A few skinny white trees give shade. There is a picnic table and, beside it, a ring of stones for a fireplace. Across the narrow gravel road is the beach and the lake.

"Better get some small, flat rocks to put under the center stands, George, or they'll dig into this soft ground and the cycles'll fall over," Hook says as I unstrap his feet. I lift him off and help him into his chair.

When I get back I place the stones. Then I help to unpack the gear and pile it on the table. Heather is walking Amie around the campsite. It will take Amie awhile to memorize the number of steps from place to place and to draw a map in her mind.

Soon the four of us are sitting on the table bench, all in a row. We each have a Coke and there's a big bag of taco chips open on Amie's lap. We are quiet, just looking out over the lake, which is bright with afternoon sun. The water laps quietly on the small sand beach and a little breeze stirs the evergreens beside us. I can hear three or four different kinds of birds. But the loudest sound is the crunching of the taco chips. Long shadows slant across the ground but the sun is still warm.

I don't feel so bad now. The sun has burned the fear away.

All the new sights and sounds mix together to make it peaceful. But as soon as I think this thought, I remember that Amie can't see the sun's rays, the shadows, or the blue lake. Heather can't hear the birds, the waves, or the breeze. Or the four of us chomping on the taco chips. And I wonder, who's luckiest? Who's most unlucky? It's like Hook says, all of us are missing something. But who's missing the most?

Later, after the chips are gone, Amie says, "Guess we should set up soon."

"You're right, Amie," Hook agrees.

I tell Heather. She and I grab the two tents and take them over to the flat spot where there is a little trench in a rectangle shape in the ground. Hook lowers himself from the bench and starts to lever himself over to us. He's the only one who knows how to put up the tents. Heather leads Amie to the spot. It would be faster if Heather and I put up the tents, with Hook telling us what to do, but that's not the way we do things.

We unroll the two little tents. Each one has a lot of strings tied to it, and a bundle of metal tubes and a bunch of small metal pegs. Hook says the tubes fit together to make two poles for each tent. We give the tubes to Amie. Amie gets to her knees and fumbles with the pole pieces, trying to join them. She feels the ends with her fingers to find out which piece fits which. Heather and I spread the tents on the ground side by side, then Hook pounds in pegs at each corner with a hatchet, dragging himself from corner to corner as he works. He holds each peg with his hook and pounds it in with the hatchet. He drops the pegs a lot. When he bangs his hook with the hatchet by mistake he yells *Ow!* and everybody laughs. When he has pegged the corners, he pounds some more pegs into the ground around the tent.

"Heather wants to know what those extra ones are for," I tell Hook.

"You'll see," he says as he drags himself closer to Amie and pounds away again.

We have to wait a bit until Amie gets the four poles put together. When that's done, we lift one of the little tents and set the poles into the two peaks. Amie holds the front steady and Hook holds the back. Heather and I stretch the pole strings out front and back and loop them around the pegs. The next step is to stretch the strings that run from the sides of each tent to another set of pegs. When we're finished tightening the strings I yell Okay and Hook and Amie let go. The tent does not fall.

"All right!" Hook yells. "We did it. One building done, one to go."

We repeat the job on the second tent. After both tents are standing, Hook tells Heather and me how to stretch a fly over the top of each one and tighten the lines. Now each tent has a double roof. If it rains, the tent roof will stay dry.

I stand and my eye is caught by the fireplace — loose rocks piled in a ring. Inside are dead ashes, a few squashed, rusted cans, and pieces of blackened tin foil. I can hear Hook and Amie talking and I see Heather walk to the picnic table. She opens a pack.

But the voices drift away as I stare at the fireplace. I feel myself kick off my shoes and peel off my socks. I drop them to the ground.

Suddenly I am loping through the soft warm sand of the beach. As I run I feel small pebbles and bits of shell scrape at my ankles. At the edge of the beach I begin to gather some dry grass. When I have a few handfuls I run farther, to the edge of the trees, and gather some dry twigs. Then some sticks about as thick as my thumbs. I pull off my

T-shirt, spread it out, then pile the stuff in it. I add some bigger pieces, wrist thick, and pick up the bundle. I head back to the empty cold fireplace, loping through the sand.

I set the fire — grass, then twigs. I build a little hut with the bigger sticks. I work slowly, carefully. A pack of matches drops beside me. I light the grass, blowing gently on it, and a finger of orange flame grows, wrapped in white smoke. Soon the small twigs are burning. The spreading flames rise to the bigger sticks.

I stand. The fire is going well. It's the way it's supposed to be. I turn and head off again, into the evergreens this time. In a few minutes I'm back with an armload of wood. I dump it beside the ring of stones and squat to tend the fire.

I can hear a voice singing in a strange language. It's a fire song, about how fire helps us, cooking our food and keeping the cold away.

It's me singing. It's my voice.

I hear a different voice behind me and I turn, still squatting. There are three people there. They are dressed strangely. Their feet are covered and their clothes are tight. One of them is moving her hands, like the old man in our village who makes shadows on the wall by moving his hands in front of a candle. He tells stories this way. But I do not understand these movements.

I feel very tired. I stand and walk past the people to the huts. The strangers watch as I pass. The huts are strange — sharp, blue shapes with lines tying them to the earth. I am too tired to care.

I crawl inside and lie down. I want to sleep. I am afraid to go outside again, afraid to close my eyes. But I want to sleep.

20

I wake feeling very hot. And my head aches.

I am wrapped in a sleeping bag and the tent is full of blue light. I hear voices — Hook's and Amie's — and the rustle of nylon as the fly moves above the tent. Something snaps and crackles. They have a fire going.

I crawl out of the bag, surprised to see I am wearing my jeans. Pushing the tent flap aside, I get out of the tent into a warm morning. Sunlight slants across the campsite and I smell smoke and fried bacon. I feel a cool, light breeze against my bare chest.

My three friends are at the table. Hook and Heather look at me, as if I was about to do something strange. The fire catches my eye. A snatch of song drifts through my head, words in another language.

"How about some grub, lazy bones?"

Hook's voice cuts the song off. Suddenly I feel starved. I sit down beside Amie. Heather pushes a plate of fried bacon to me and another piled with toast. Amie gets up and moves slowly to the camp stove on the end of the table. Carefully, she pours a cup of tea.

I look around. The lake is a hard blue. The sun on the water is so bright it hurts my eyes a little. The fire pops and birds are talking in the branches.

I build a bacon sandwich and gulp some of the warm tea.

"You okay?" Amie asks as she sits down beside me.

"Yeah," I say past a mouthful of food. "Did I go away last night?"

"Sure did. Missed a good supper, too."

"No sweat," Hook cuts in. "All the more for me." He turns his face to Heather beside him. "Heather didn't tell us what a great cook she is. Terrific spaghetti sauce."

I am making my second sandwich. Heather's hands move.

"No, I didn't have The Dream last night," I answer. "I didn't dream at all."

"You sure devoted yourself to that fire, George Horse," Hook says. "Absolutely. You remember that?"

My eyes flip over to the ring of stones. "Sort of."

I think for a minute. "At home, it was my job to get the fire going every morning."

"What was that song you were singing?" Amie asks.

"Song?"

"Yeah. It went like this." She hums for a little bit.

The same snatch of song comes alive in my head again. "It's a fire song the villagers sing." I tell them about it, as much as I remember.

"It sounded nice," Hook says. "Nice tune. Made me wish I was Chinese, too."

"Oh, that wasn't Chinese."

Hook and Heather look confused. Beside me, Amie asks, "How many languages *can* you speak, then?"

"Umm. My father was — or is — Chinese. Born in North China, I mean. We talked Chinese between ourselves. I guess he wanted me to know it. But our village in —"

"Southeast Asia somewhere," Hook cuts in.

"Yeah. That's where I was born. So I guess I speak two languages. Or used to."

"Plus English. Plus signing," Heather's hands add.

"How about singing the whole song for us, George?" Amie asks quietly.

"Yeah," Hook puts in.

They are watching me. My eyes cut to the fire again. I begin to sing, real quiet. All the words come easily. When I'm finished, no one says anything. I realize there are tears on my cheeks.

Heather looks away. Hook is staring at his plate, moving a couple of crusts around with his hook. Amie gets up and pours herself more tea.

Hook looks up. "Hey, George, check out the campsite. Just like home, right?"

I look around, more carefully this time, wondering what Hook means. Slowly, one by one, I notice the changes. The cycles have been moved from the big rock to the edge of the evergreens at the back of our campsite. They look like motorcycles again — all the gear has been stripped off. They sit under the orange tarps that have been tied to some white trees on an angle. They look like little tents. Near the picnic table two mirrors are hung from another white tree — Amie says they're called birches. One mirror is only three feet off the ground. That must be Hook's. And there's a rope from the mirror tree to another birch. A couple of towels are pegged to the rope.

The campsite looks . . . better now. Not so scary. The wall of evergreens has patches of color — blue, orange, yellow — showing against it. People colors, not forest colors. Then I laugh.

Because I catch sight of the sign nailed to the edge of the picnic table. It's a blue sign, just like the one on the washroom door at school.

I laugh again. "The Cripples' Campsite," I say.

"Right on," returns Hook. "Absolutely."

馬

It is afternoon. Yellow bars of sunlight slant across the campsite. The road and beach and lake are still brightly lit. Hook and I are sitting at the table, facing the blue lake, sipping Cokes. Heather and Amie are out on the road, making a map in Amie's head.

This morning Heather and I took turns leading Amie around the campsite, back and forth. From the table — the "center" — to the cycles. From the table to the tents. From the table to the road. Amie would murmur quietly to herself, counting steps, feeling with her cane. After a while she could do it herself pretty easily. She memorized the layout and made a map in her head. But she still has to go carefully because of all the roots that poke up out of the ground.

"I'm so good at this," she laughed, "that I could do it in the dark!"

Now she is working on the road — to the bathroom, to the beach.

Hook is looking at a map, too. It's spread out on the picnic table. A compass sits on the paper.

It is hot out but Hook is not wearing shorts like the rest of us. He says he can't. He can't feel if he is getting sunburned. And he can't tell if a mosquito is biting him. So he has to wear long pants for protection.

"Besides," he told me in the tent earlier, "I'm not real

proud of these skinny white stick legs of mine."

Now he taps the map with his hook. "Come on over here and look at this, George."

I move to his side. Under his hook is a big patch of blue, showing bright against the white background.

"This is our lake. Here's the shore — the south shore — where we're camped. Right now, we're looking due north. Here's the beach." He looks up and points to the biggest island. Then he taps the map again. "And out there is Sugarloaf Island."

Then he adds, "Look at this," and runs his finger back and forth over the paper. "Nothing but forest for miles and miles and miles. Nothing around us — except for the highway ten miles back — except wilderness."

Hook looks at me, right in my eyes. "It's like being in the middle of the jungle."

I turn the map toward me a little. A shadow from the mirror birch falls across the big white area that Hook was pointing at. Empty forest. Jungle.

"I still think it's a goofy idea," Amie complains as she digs her fork into the noodles and cheese on her plate. She winds the noodles against a spoon.

"Naw, it'll be great," Hook answers, "right, Heather?"

"I'm all for it," she signs. Heather has cut her noodles up into little bits. She eats them with a spoon. Hook and Amie always kid her about it. She eats spaghetti this way, too.

Hook slurps at a long noodle that dangles from his mouth and slowly rises up to his face. Just before it disappears it flips, splashing cheese onto the end of his nose.

"How gross!" Heather signs. I pass on what she says.

"Hook, you got no class."

"He probably has cheese all over his ugly puss by now. Right, George?" Amie asks. The sinking sun flashes in her mirrors.

"Yes, Amie."

"George, what's your opinion?" Hook asks, ignoring Amie.

Heather's hands fly while she gives out her hiss-laugh. "He already gave his opinion. You've got cheese all over your face. I hope a bear licks it clean tonight so we don't have to look at it tomorrow."

After I translate, Hook laughs, too, then asks, "Really, Horse, what do you think?"

Hook wants me to agree with him. He always does. But so does Amie. "I don't even know what a ganoose is. But I guess it's okay with me."

"*Canoe*," says Amie. "George, you never paddled a boat where you came from?"

"I don't think so."

Hook wants to cycle back to Canoe Lake tomorrow and rent two *canoes* so we can paddle around for a while. He'll show us how to do it. "If we can ride two Triumphs," he repeated while supper was cooking, "then canoes will be absolutely no problem. We are the Cripples' Club, and we are magnificent."

I don't want to do it. I am afraid of the water. Walking along the beach up to my knees in the cold lake was okay. But I don't want to go out on the waves in a boat. I'm afraid of The Well. And if I go I'll have The Dream at night. I am hoping Amie will win the argument.

"Let's do it," I translate for Heather. "It'll be fun. If it isn't, we'll push Hook in the lake and leave him there." Then she goes *hiss, hiss, hiss*.

"I suppose," Amie says to him, "you'll want to be captain."

"Absolutely!" he cries. "Captain Hook. You know, like in *Peter Pan*?"

"Yeah, well, you know what happened to *him*, don't you?"

"Yeah, he found some treasure."

Heather jumps in, "No chance. Amie means, he got eaten by an alligator!"

I don't know what an alligator is, but I try to laugh along with the girls. Heather's *hiss* is going on and on, and she slaps the table with her palm. Amie is going into her Giggle.

Hook's voice rises over Amie's laugh. "Since you guys all agreed to the canoe caper, I'm going to give you a reward. I've been saving this news for a special occasion."

Heather's hissing and Amie's Giggle keep going.

"Well, don't you want to know what it is?" Hook tries again.

"Yeah, sure," Amie manages to say. "Out with it."

Heather's hands agree. "Come on, spill it."

"All right," Hook smiles. "I suppose I'll tell you. I was talking to my uncle on the phone last week. Guess who got arrested awhile ago?"

"Santa Claus?" Heather signs, just as Amie shouts, "The Tooth Fairy! Come on, mystery man, cut the dramatics!"

Hook laughs.

"Silverheels," I say.

Hook looks at me. "Right on, George Horse. They got him for pushing. And they made it stick this time. Absolutely."

"It's about time," Amie says, her voice hard. "I hope he got a hundred years."

"Well, wait 'til you hear side B," Hook says. "You're gonna love this. Instead of sending him to jail, the judge gave him a choice — jail or community service." He throws his head back and laughs.

"What's *that*?"

Heather's hands begin to fly and I talk fast to keep up. "I know about that. They had a woman at my old school for the deaf who was doing something like that. Sometimes a judge gets the person who is in trouble with the law to do something in the community to help people. The person has to be at work every day and not get into any more trouble — stuff like that. It's supposed to be a way for the person to sort of pay back society for whatever crime he did. It's supposed to be more positive than jail."

"Yeah, well, I guess *anything* is more positive than jail," Amie puts in.

Hook is impatient to say more. "But guess what old Kevin Silverheels Ross is doing? He's working in a halfway house for alcoholics. He's the janitor and general cleaner-upper or something. My uncle said he *asked* for that job, specifically. He made it very clear to the judge that's what he wanted to do."

After a minute Amie says, "Hook, how come you think that's funny? I think it's good."

"So do I. I wasn't laughing at *him*. I was laughing at — I don't know. It's funny sometimes, the way things turn out. I used to hate the guy, and now I sort of feel sorry for him."

I know what Hook means. I remember when we went to get the cycle back. Silverheels shoving his mother into the house after she threw the can of beer at him. Hook means that, in a way, Silverheels is a cripple, too.

"Well, your Lowness — I mean, your *Highness*," Amie says after a few minutes, "your turn to wash, my turn to dry. Let's get at it."

She drops her fork onto her empty plate. The sharp clatter makes me jump. I have been looking out over the lake. Nothing but waves, for miles and miles and miles.

21

I don't like it on this island.

It is about the size of two of the gyms at school and shaped like an upside down bowl. It's mostly gray rock, with a few tall pine trees and some low bushes. Moss and grass grow wherever there are seams and cracks in the rock.

From the little rocky bay where we are we can see our campsite down the lake, the white beach and small patches of blue — our tents.

Yesterday, Hook and Heather cycled back to Canoe Lake Outfitters and rented two canoes. The outfitters delivered them this morning in an old pickup truck, along with four paddles and four life jackets. The canoes are made of some kind of metal, fifteen feet long, and silver colored. There's a picture of a deer's head on the front of each one.

It took a long time to get here from the campsite because

we don't know how to paddle very well. Hook can't paddle at all. He tried, but his hook wouldn't hold the paddle. He even tried to tie the paddle to the hook, but it wouldn't work. So he sat on the floor in the front and I sat in the back. He had to sit low because he can't feel anything in his legs and that makes it hard to keep his balance up on the seat. He said he was "top heavy."

I couldn't steer the canoe right. First we'd go to the right, then to the left. Hook told me to change sides, so when we went left, I'd paddle on the left. Then the canoe would swing and point the other way. Heather had the same trouble so as we crossed the flat calm water to this island, the canoes kept banging together, making a hollow, tinny sound. Hook and the girls laughed a lot and splashed each other. One time Amie said, "You'd think *I* was steering this thing!"

I didn't laugh.

Our canoe was tippy and I was always scared we'd flip over. The canoe seemed to go where it wanted to.

And I don't know how to swim.

As soon as we got here, I made a fire and we roasted hot dogs on sticks for lunch. Heather kept calling them "charcoal dogs" and "cinder dogs" because we didn't cook them too well.

Amie is up on the highest part of the rock now, leaning against a tree, reading. Her pink T-shirt shows up bright against the blue sky. Her thin black fingers slip across the pages, back and forth, back and forth. The breeze flips her hair and riffles the pages of the book.

Hook is in the shade down the rock a bit, stretched out on three orange life jackets with the fourth for a pillow. He is snoring.

A few minutes ago Heather wanted to dump a can of lake water on him, but she and I were too lazy. I'm sitting on a boulder at the lake shore under the hot sun, watching

Heather swim. She's good. Her long white arms cut through the calm water of the bay, leaving a smooth wake behind her as she glides back and forth. She's been at it for almost an hour.

I look at the long silver bottoms of the overturned canoes. I wish I could swim.

"Hey!" It's Amie's voice. I turn to look. "It's getting windy up here," she shouts.

My eye travels up the tall trunk of the pine tree she's leaning against. The green top is bending and straightening as the wind sighs through the branches. I look back down the lake toward our campsite. Past the bay where Heather is swimming, the lake is not calm.

"Maybe we should head back," Amie yells. "Hey! Am I talking to myself, or what?"

"What's the screaming about?" Hook asks, sitting up, rubbing his eyes with his hand. He is wearing a baggy green bathing suit with red frogs hopping all over it.

"A guy comes up to the Great White North to get some peace and quiet," he goes on, "and all he hears is skinny little black girls stretching their lungs."

"What's that?" Amie calls out.

"Nothing. I was just insulting you."

"What else is new? Well, you going to come up here and check out the wind, or what?"

"Okay, okay. Keep your shirt on," Hook says. "I'll just stroll right up there."

"I'm not wearing a shirt."

"In that case, I'll gallop right up there."

Amie giggles. "Pervert!"

Heather is wading out of the water, carefully. It's hard to walk on the slippery rocks. I tell her what Amie wants. She slips into her running shoes, drying herself with a big towel. Then she pulls on a white T-shirt with a picture of the CN Tower on it.

Hook has already levered himself backwards up the sloping rock to Amie's tree when Heather and I get there. "Oh, oh," Hook says.

Up here the wind is strong and steady. It's a lot cooler, too. All around us, the tea-colored lake is choppy and there are flecks of white on the waves.

"Look." He points up to the north end of the lake. The sky in the distance is darkening and there's a dull gray smudge along the treetops.

Hook describes what we see to Amie and then adds, "I think we'd better hit the road, gang. That's a storm coming."

"Road?" laughs Amie, folding a page over and closing her thick book.

Heather's hands answer. "Hook never was good at metaphors." I pass it on.

Hook doesn't laugh. He doesn't even smile. He keeps looking out over the lake. "Let's get moving."

I'm looking at the gray line on the sky. "Maybe we should stay here until the storm passes."

Amie is on her feet now, with her hand on Heather's shoulder, ready to walk.

"There's no protection on this island, George," says Hook.

"Yeah, and all our stuff is lying around the campsite," Amie adds. "If it rains, we'll have wet clothes, wet food, wet everything." The joking tone is gone.

Heather does not see what Amie is saying. "The tent flaps are tied open," she signs. "The rain will get in."

I squat down and Hook wraps his arms around me. I reach back and hook my arms under his legs and stand. We follow Heather as she slowly leads Amie down to the boats.

"It'll be okay," Hook is saying. "We'll be going *with* the wind and waves and the campsite is only a half mile or so down the lake. It won't take long. If we had to go *against* the wind we'd be up a creek."

"You messed up your metaphor again," Amie says.

I lower Hook onto the boulder I was sitting on earlier, then roll the boats over and drag them into the shallow water. Heather runs around, picking up our stuff, tossing Hook's and my shirts to us, stuffing our other things into a pack. She tosses the pack to me and I drop it into our canoe. She drops two life jackets and two paddles into each boat. Each time something hits the bottom of a canoe it makes a hollow thumping sound, like a drum.

Heather wades between the boats and holds them steady while I carry Hook to the front of our boat and help him in. Then I lead Amie into the water and hold her arm while she steps into the front of her canoe and sits down. Her lips are pressed tight together and she clutches the paddle when I put it into her hands.

I wade back. Heather lets go of our canoe and quickly signs, "Stay together!"

I nod, then step carefully into the boat. It wobbles and jerks, then settles when I sit down. I pick up my paddle and look back. Heather has climbed into her boat. I dig the blade of my paddle into the water and the boat starts to move.

The canoe makes its crooked way across the bay. As it moves I get more and more afraid. I know the wind and waves will take us over. On land, we can all help each other. Here, what will we do? Amie can't see where she's going. She has already started yelling, "Where are you guys?" every few minutes in a tense voice. Heather and I can't steer properly. Hook's strong arms can't help us.

And I can't swim.

We move slowly. Heather and I have to keep changing sides so the boats will not go in circles. The canoes bump together at times, making a hollow boom. No one laughs.

Once we get out of the bay we are surrounded by the roaring wind and we start to feel the swell of the waves that push us from behind. Now we have to struggle and fight, switching sides fast and often, to keep the boats straight. If we get turned sideways to the waves we'll roll over.

After a while I start to get tired. The waves are worse. They are big and wide and dark, with white foam on the top. They come at us from behind, lifting the canoe up, shoving us forward, rolling underneath with a long, snarling splash, then lowering us.

I take a quick look back. The gray line in the sky is darker and thicker. There's an ugly purple patch way in the distance, like a bruise, close to the lake. Where we are, it's still sunny.

The wind is stronger. It whips spray off the tops of the waves and soon my back is wet and cold. The waves are bigger now, and closer together. Before one wave drops us down, another hits the back of the canoe, slopping water in. The waves slide under us two at a time, splashing along the edges of the canoes, dumping water in.

I dig hard into the moving water. My arms and shoulders ache. My back aches. I look over at Heather. She is soaked. Her red hair is plastered to her head. Her T-shirt sticks to her like skin. Her frightened face stands out white against the dark water behind her. Amie is soaked, too. Her small body pumps up and down as she digs deep with the paddle.

They have separated from us a bit but they're close enough that I can see a lot of water sloshing around in their boat. Every wave adds more. Our boat has a lot of water inside, too. The two orange life jackets wash back and forth, from me to Hook and back again, as the boat rises and falls.

"Where are you guys?" Amie yells for the hundredth time.

"We're here, about ten feet away," Hook shouts back.

"How close are we?"

"About half way."

"Oh God, is that all?" Amie's words come out in gasps. "Hook, I can't keep this up. Can't we rest?"

"I got an idea," he shouts. He waves to Heather. I know what he wants. He wants to get the boats together.

I switch and paddle hard on the left. Heather gets the idea, too, and paddles on her right. The rocking canoes come close together and Hook shouts to Amie to lift her paddle. The boats bang against each other, almost knocking Amie out with the shock, and Hook leans over to grab the support bar of Amie's seat. But because of the shape of the boats, the back ends are forced apart and a wave rolls through between us. When the canoes lift, Hook loses his hold.

"Try it again!" Hook yells. The wind whips his words away. He lies back in the water on the bottom of our boat, reaches up and behind to grab the crossbar, and drags himself under it. Then he sits up and levers himself back to the center crossbar and leans against it. Water drips from the back of his head.

Heather and I are paddling furiously, trying to bring the boats together again. A wave lifts and drops us, slopping water in, and as we drop, the boats thump together again. Hook grabs the center crossbar of the girls' boat. The muscles bulge under his soaked red shirt.

"George, are your jeans in the pack?"

"Yeah, I think so."

"Get 'em, quick!"

Holding my paddle with one hand, I reach forward and drag the little pack to me. I rip open the straps, yank out the stuff — books, a bag of hot dog buns, a tea pot, towels — dropping things into the water at my feet. I toss the jeans to Hook.

He uses the legs of the pants to tie the boats together, using his teeth, his hand, his hook to make a fat blue knot.

"Okay," he shouts against the wind, "This should be better. George, just concentrate on keeping us straight, okay? If you see us going right, tell Amie to paddle hard. Amie, don't paddle unless George says." He says nothing to Heather because she can't see his face.

But she has the idea. For a while, it works. We don't need to paddle quite as hard. The two canoes are like a raft, blown and shoved down the lake. We are making pretty good speed without having to work as hard. The campsite looks a lot closer.

The only trouble is the water sloshing in. The waves roll under us making a fountain between the boats and dumping water in. The more water we get, the lower the canoes sit and the easier it is for the next wave to get in. And we seem to be going slower even though the wind is strong.

Hook notices, too. "George, kick that teapot to me."

I pick it out of the water and hand it to him. He leans over the knot and starts bailing water from the girls' boat. When he throws a pot full of water over the far side, the wind snatches it and turns it into spray before it can hit the waves.

The wind is blowing so hard now that when I lift my paddle between strokes I can feel it pushing against the blade. Water keeps spraying up between the canoes and raining into them. But I think Hook is gaining as he bails.

Then a big wave lifts me so fast and so high I lose my balance and fall back. My elbows bash against the edges of the canoe and my arms and hands go numb. My paddle falls into the boat. The two canoes lift up high. But the girls' is lighter because it has less water in it now. At the top of the wave, the jeans stretch tightly, then with a loud *r-r-r-ipppp!* the boats jerk apart. The girls' boat takes a crazy rock sideways. Amie loses her balance. Her paddle flies out of her hand as she falls back and to the side, banging her head hard against the edge of the canoe as she pitches out of the boat.

Amie begins to sink away behind us. Unmoving. Face up in the dark water. Heather moves fast. In one motion she scrabbles forward and grabs the tie-string of one of the life jackets that's washing around in the boat. She stands. Wobbles for a second. Plunges into the waves near Amie. The water closes over her head and she disappears.

A few seconds later she comes up, still holding the life jacket by the string.

"Heather's coming, Amie. Heather's coming!" It's my voice.

Heather fights against the waves, swimming with one hand. Amie's legs and arms begin to move. Heather clutches the pink cloth of Amie's T-shirt behind her head. Amie's arms thrash the water and she lifts her head high, gasping. Her mirror glasses are gone.

I dig in hard with my paddle, trying to move the canoe toward the girls. Hook snatches the spare paddle as it floats past him and holds it out toward Heather. But Heather has the life jacket in one hand and the other is twisted into Amie's shirt.

"Amie!" Hook screams. "Reach out in front of you! Grab the paddle!"

But Amie has lost control. Her arms thrash the water in front of her, and she is screaming, screaming like a hurt animal.

Heather is struggling to hang onto her. A wave rolls over them. Amie comes up coughing. Hook yells again but Amie only thrashes and screams. Suddenly, Hook lunges to get the paddle closer to them. And when he does, the boat tips way off center and the wave that is passing under us pours into the boat, swamping us completely.

"Hang on, George!" Hook calls out as he rolls over the edge of the canoe. He swims a couple of strokes, dragging his white stick-legs behind him. He grabs a handful of cloth on Amie's T-shirt. He and Heather start hauling her toward our boat. Heather's boat has drifted out of reach, surfing easily on the waves now that it is empty. Our boat is hardly moving.

As they come toward me, I can feel the boat begin to sink under me. The back end where I am sitting is already under water. The two life jackets are picked up by a wave and float off. Hook slams his hook over the edge of the canoe at the front and pulls Amie to him. Heather lets go of her and grabs the edges, too. Hook takes Amie's arm and presses her hand against the metal.

Amie has stopped screaming and thrashing. She understands, and holds on with both hands. Hook is talking to her as he pushes the life jacket over her head. Heather sees what he's doing and, letting go of the canoe, she takes the strings of the life jacket and ties them around Amie's waist.

Hook says something to Amie and I think I see her nod. Then he turns to face Heather and talks to her. She nods and starts working her way arm over arm to where I am. Hook flounders into the swamped boat, across it, and out the other side. He hangs onto the edge opposite Amie.

Then he looks at me. "George! Get in the water across from Heather and hold on like she is."

Heather is looking up at me. Hook yells again. "George, it's all right! Get into the water and hang on. The canoe won't sink if you do that."

But I am beginning to slip away.

The black waves are rolling and tossing around me. The wind howls as the waves try to swallow the boat and swallow me. Near me, three bodies float on the water.

Waves wash over them, trying to pull them down.

Something flips in my mind and I know this has happened to me before. The others are lost now. This time I will not fight the waves. I don't care any more.

Something strong wraps around my waist and pulls me over the side. I give up. I let go of the paddle. A wave crashes over me and I start to sink. Down and down.

But my head breaks the surface again. I hear a voice. Then a stinging slap on my face. The slap knocks the breath out of me. Water splashes in my face, making me cough and splutter. Something grips my hand and bangs it against metal. I hold on, hard.

The voice again. Angry. Angrier than the howling wind. It's Hook. *"We are gonna get through this, dammit! We are not gonna let this beat us!"*

The gray cloud has taken over the sky, covered up the sun. The purple bruise on the cloud is huge. The four of us are clutching the swamped canoe.

I start to kick my feet.

22

After a long, long time, the canoe hits something and shudders. We are at the beach.

Heather's canoe is already here, rolling and pitching in the waves.

I stand up, waist deep in the water. The wind is cold on my back. The waves breaking on the beach try to push me over. Heather stands, too. Then Amie. No one says anything.

I wade to Hook and squat in the water in front of him. His arms loop around my shoulders. I hook my arms around his stick legs and struggle to stand. I can barely make it.

The three of us stagger up the beach, across the road, into our campsite. I lower Hook onto the seat of the picnic table and drop down beside him. The girls plop down on the seat across from us, facing the lake. Amie takes off her life jacket and drops it to the ground. It makes a squashy sound when it hits.

"We," says Hook in a tired voice, "are *invincible*."

"Yeah, well, I don't *feel* invincible," Amie says, rubbing the back of her head.

"Me either," Heather signs. I pass it on.

We sit quietly for a few minutes, breathing deep tired breaths.

"Look at this place!" Heather's hands say.

When I translate, we look around. The tents have blown down, and one of the flies, with only one rope holding it, is whipping around like a blue kite. The tarps that covered the cycles are torn loose and they jerk and snap in the wind like orange flags. There's dust and sticks and old dead leaves blowing all over the place. The wind carries spray from the crashing waves right into the campsite.

"I'm cold," Amie complains.

"No wonder," Hook says. "We look like rats that've been out in the rain for a year."

"Speaking of rain," Heather signs, "look at that sky. We'd better get set up again."

I pass it on, then look where she's pointing. The bruise on the sky has turned to black and the lake is so dark we can hardly see the island we were on.

"Come on, George." Heather slowly gets to her feet.

I don't bother to translate. I follow her to the nearest tent and we each pick up a pole, set it straight, and tighten the lines. Then we go around the walls and tighten all the other lines. We do the same to the second tent. Then we put the fly back over each one. The wind rips and tears at the tents and snaps the flies up and down.

"Let's get some rocks to hold everything down," she signs.

I nod and start searching. I bring rocks from the edge of the beach to the picnic table and drop them. Heather rolls them into place — at the tent corners and on the lines where they are tied to the pegs. While we're working, Hook and Amie are inside the tents putting on dry clothes. When we're finished, it's our turn. Then we go back to the table to join them.

"Hey!" Hook says. "We forgot something. The canoes."

Heather rolls her eyes and she and I get to our feet again. We walk down to the beach and haul the boats up onto the sand. It's hard to roll them over because of all the water inside. We go back and sit down. She lets out a long, tired breath.

We sit for a while, bundled up in all our warm clothing. Three of us watch the black cloud work its way down the lake toward us. The wind is not so strong now. But it's getting dark.

"Thanks guys." Amie's voice.

I look at her face. She looks different without her mirrors. Stronger.

"What?" Hook says, turning to face her.

"You guys saved my life out there."

Heather puts her arm around Amie's shoulder, then takes it away to sign.

"Heather says she thinks we all saved each other."

I know it's not true. I was useless. But I say nothing.

Amie nods. "Well, maybe."

"Absolutely right," Hook puts in. After a minute, he goes on. "You know, that's the difference between us and some other people. They take care of themselves. We take care of each other."

Heather and Amie nod. Heather picks at the table top with a finger nail.

Hook talks again. "Now, let's get inside. The rain's coming, I'm totally worn out, and I've already been wet once today."

I am in the tent, in my sleeping bag. The rainstorm has come. Light flashes suddenly. A few seconds later, *Crack! Boom!* The ground under the tent shakes as if it was afraid.

A voice cuts the darkness. "You all right, George?"

"The storm is making me feel bad."

"Well, try not to worry. It's just a lot of air bashing around up there." Hook gives out a long yawn. "We've had a hell of a day, but we survived."

The rain has started. Sound of a long, never-ending breath. As if the forest was breathing.

For a long time I stare up into the darkness that fills the tent. Hook's deep, even breathing tells me he's asleep. Outside, the gusts snatch at the fly and punch the tent walls. Trying to get in. The thunder rumbles and cracks, like a steel ball rolling on a wood floor. The lightning stabs into the tent. It hurts my eyes.

I can feel myself starting to slip away. I knew it would happen. I clutch the edge of my sleeping bag. Squeeze. But it is no use. Something in my mind opens up, as if a curtain was pulled aside.

I have to get out of the hut. It's time now. Time to go. Father said we leave tonight. He will be waiting with my sisters.

I crawl from the hut into the blackness. I stand. The rain is warm on my skin. I walk across the clearing, away from the village.

Into the jungle.

23

Explosions pound around us as we crouch under the dark trees at the edge of the trail. Orange flashes in the black jungle. The rain roars, beating the leaves.

One of the children jumps up and runs down the narrow trail. Disappears quickly. A voice behind me yells.

"No! Stop!"

Down the trail a different explosion — poom!

We stumble out of the jungle into a clearing. The bamboo huts are burned black, beaten down by the rain.

There are bodies scattered, bloated and pale. Some wear uniforms. Most wear black villagers' clothing. The smell of rot is a heavy fog.

I stop at the edge of a paddy. I recognize the naked child lying at the edge of the shallow dirty water. Leg twisted

*under her. One side of her burnt black. Empty eyes staring
into the low sky. Rain drives like nails into the eyes. She
shouldn't be here. She should be on the trail.*

*I step into the paddy, stand over her. A rat swims away. I
feel vomit creep into the back of my throat.*

The child's head moves.

The small mouth opens.

"You." A cracked voice over broken teeth.

*"No, no!" I back away. My feet slide on the yellow clay
of the paddy dike. I fall. Scrabble to my feet again, out of
the paddy.*

*The dead child rolls onto her stomach. She drags herself
out of the water and onto the path. The hand is missing
from the burned arm. The fingers of the other hand dig
into the clay.*

She whispers.

"You. It was you."

*She lowers her head and crawls toward me, dragging
her burned leg. Her long black hair is matted with clay.
Her little head lifts again. Her empty slanted eyes stare.*

"It's your fault. Yours!"

*"No! No! No-o-o-o-o-o," my voice rises, louder and
louder. It becomes thunder, pounding in my ears.*

The child's corpse dissolves in the rain.

*Thunder cracks and booms over the ship. Yellow-white
forks of lightning in the purple sky.*

*The ship rears and plunges. Rain comes sideways,
stinging. Waves boil over the sides of the ship, washing
across the decks. Washing people overboard. The girl is
ripped from my arms by the waves. Screaming.*

*The ship is blind. Dying. Waves climb higher. White
foam on the tops of the waves is ripped away by the wind.*

The wind screams, from a black mouth, over broken teeth. Faces float on the waves, black mouths open. Voices scream out of the faces.

"You! Your fault! Yours!"

Then another voice. "I'm sorry! I'm sorry! I'm sorry!"

"George!"

"I'm sorry!"

Voices.

Voices from the wind. Voices from the waves. My voice. More voices.

I am drowning. Drowning in the voices.

24

"I think I can tell you now. I think I can remember."

We are sitting on logs around the fire. Hook says, even though it's a warm morning with a bright sun, that we have to have a fire. There's a teapot sitting on one of the rocks beside the flames.

"That's great, George," he says. "Whenever you're ready." He smiles.

Water still drips from the trees and the ground is wet. There's a nice, fresh smell in the air.

Amie nods. "You sure gave us a scare, George." She takes a sip of tea.

"Yeah," Hook cuts in. "Know where we found you?" He points across the clearing toward the big rock. "Right there, under that Christmas tree. You were lying on the ground, all curled up."

"Amie and Hook heard you yelling," Heather's hands go on. "Amie woke me up and we crawled out of bed to see what was wrong. It was pouring rain. Lots of lightning, too. Amie followed your voice and led me over to you — I couldn't see a thing, it was so dark."

"You were soaked, George Horse. You looked like you went swimming!"

Amie talks again. "It was spooky."

"I'm sorry, Amie."

"No, that's not what I meant. In a way, it was *good*, wasn't it?"

Heather's hands again. "Yeah. It was good for you, right, George? But it hurt a lot, didn't it?"

I nod. Heather's blue eyes show me that she knows. She knows what it was like, sort of. Even though it didn't happen to her.

They all know — Heather, Amie, Hook. It didn't happen to them. But other things did.

The sun feels good on my back. I can hear birds talking in the branches. The tiny fire pops and cracks.

Then, without thinking, I start to talk.

For a long time before we left White Crane village Father tried to get the villagers to run away. He said that our village grew a lot more rice than most, and that would mean that both sides would try to control us. Sooner or later we would have to choose sides, and then we would be in the war.

But no one wanted to run away. Where would we go? they asked.

Then he tried to get them to send the children away. He offered to take them himself. How could we live without our children? they asked.

I remember Father arguing lots of times with the other Elders of the village. No one would listen. So one night he told my two sisters and me to get ready to leave the next night. But we couldn't tell anyone.

"You had two sisters?" Amie cuts in. "I didn't know that!"

"What's this about soldiers, George?" Heather's hands say. "Who was your country fighting against?"

After I pass this on I say, "It wasn't against anyone outside. I think."

"A civil war," Amie adds.

"Hey, I got an idea," Hook says. "Let's let George tell this his way, then ask questions later."

Heather and Amie agree and I start up again.

The night we left it was pouring rain. Like last night. When the village was asleep we sneaked away into the dark. We took two bundles — food, some extra clothes, some bedding — and left everything else behind.

Father had a rope with four knots in it. He led, I was last, and my two sisters were between us. Spring was eight. She was chubby and wore her hair in long braids that came down past her waist. Little Monkey was six. She was tiny and very thin, but full of energy and fun. Her real name was Long Happiness, but that name was too big for her.

It rained constantly. The jungle was black-dark and the trails were narrow and twisting. Soon after we left the village we were in the mountains. It was hard going, especially for my sisters. One would slip in the wet clay and fall, pulling down the other, because they were too scared to let go of the rope. After a few hours Father and I would take turns carrying Little Monkey on our backs.

Sometimes we would come to a narrow road in a valley. We could not cross until Father had lugged heavy branches to the road and thrown them across the track. Then he would find a longer thinner branch and go across slowly, poking the dirt ahead of him, as far as he could reach. When he got to the other side he would let us cross, one by one. But we had to step in his footsteps. It was hard to see them in the dark.

When we saw daylight we would slip off the trail into the trees. Father and I would build a little shelter to help keep the rain off. We would eat cold rice and then go to sleep. We were scared, but we fell asleep easily.

I stop talking and take a sip of cold tea.

"What was your dad doing at the roads?" ask Heather's hands.

After I translate Hook cuts in, "I know. Land mines, right George?"

"Yes. The first time he did it he explained it to me and my sisters. The soldiers buried mines in the roads and the wide trails. If you stepped on one, it would explode. But not right away. When you stepped on one you would hear a loud *click*. Then, when you lifted your foot off it, it would blow up."

On the fourth night the rain let up. We were stumbling and slipping along, holding tight to the rope. Suddenly Father stopped. Little Monkey and Spring sat down right away. They were tired. I knew it was too soon for a rest stop so I asked Father what was wrong.

"Shhhh!" was all he said. I listened. The jungle dripped around us.

Then I smelled smoke.

"Soldiers!" Father hissed. He yanked hard on the rope and my sisters jumped to their feet. He led us back along the trail the way we had come, then cut into the jungle. It was hard to see. We hid under a big deadfall. Father told us to stay there while he had a look around.

While he was gone we huddled together, straining to hear. Spring and Little Monkey were terrified. Night by night homesickness and fear had been filling them up. I could feel their terror.

I was scared, too. I was sure every plop of rain from the trees above us was a soldier's boot on the jungle floor. Then I did hear someone moving in the dark. My sisters and I crawled deeper under the deadfall.

"It's me. I'm back."

It was Father. He crawled under and came close to whisper. His voice floated out of the dark. "Yes, it's soldiers. I didn't expect this. The war must be hotter than I thought. Normally the soldiers wouldn't use these trails — too narrow and difficult. It must be a patrol. They're Browns. We'll wait here until they move on. It's too risky to try to go around them. Besides, this trail is the quickest way."

He moved closer and hugged Little Monkey and Spring. "Don't worry. We'll be safe."

We got as comfortable as we could and settled down. The children were too scared to sleep, so Father told them a Chinese story about the Monkey King and the White Boned Demon. *Sūn Wŭkōng* — the Monkey King — was Little Monkey's favorite. He lived on the Mountain of Flowers and Fruit with his followers. He was magic and a great fighter. He carried a little pin in his ear and when he was fighting he would take it out and turn it into a bamboo fighting staff. Little Monkey used to play *Sūn Wŭkōng*. That's where she got her nickname.

So, even though she was scared, Little Monkey was soon laughing quietly at the story. Father was a good story-teller. He would change his voice and play all the parts.

But I sat staring into the black jungle, watching and listening for soldiers.

The soldiers did not move on. More came the next day. So Father and I dug a big hole under the deadfall. We cut branches for a floor because water soon ran into it. And we cut more branches to stick in the ground in front of the deadfall to hide it.

It rained all day. It was miserable in the hole. At night the rain stopped. Father told another story while we ate our rice and dried fruit. After that we settled down to sleep.

Then a giant thunderclap smashed against our eardrums and the ground shook. My sisters shrieked out loud. Another roar came, with a flash of light.

But it wasn't thunder.

"Mortar shells!" Father hissed. It was the start of a battle, and we were in the middle of it.

The Grays and Browns fought all night. Red and orange flashed in the jungle over and over. The ground shook. It was like a giant was slamming his hand onto the ground over and over, right beside our hiding place. My sisters lay curled up on the floor of the hole, whimpering. Father and I sat for hours, leaning against the sides of the hole, with our hands pressed over our ears.

When dawn came the machine guns started to rattle. Sometimes we heard bullets whining through the air above. Then something exploded close to us and lumps of earth and sticks rained down on the deadfall.

Little Monkey shrieked. Suddenly, before we knew what was happening, she was up on her feet. She scrabbled out of the hole.

"No!" Father yelled. But she was running toward the trail. Father and I scrambled from the hole and ran after her. At the edge of the trail he tripped on a root and fell flat. I ran out onto the trail and stopped. Which way did Little Monkey go? My head snapped back and forth as I looked up and down the narrow trail.

"Go right!" Father shouted. "I'll go left!"

I ran, sliding downhill. After a few seconds I caught sight of a flutter of black cloth at a turning in the trail. I made the corner. The trail was almost straight here, following a little gully.

I saw her.

"Monkey, stop!" I called.

Just then she slipped and her feet shot out from under her. She slammed hard onto her back and lay there for a second. Then she slowly rolled over and got up onto her hands and knees.

I stopped. "Don't run!" I yelled.

Her panic seemed to have disappeared. She stood up. Her long black hair was matted with yellow clay, and clay streaked her face. She wiped her hands on her dirty black pants. Her tiny chest was heaving.

Her eyes were wide, but she smiled. She looked . . . embarrassed. She took a step toward me, holding out her arms.

Click!

The smile dropped from her face. Her eyes got wider. "Brother, help!" she whimpered.

"No, don't —"

She tried to run to me.

The explosion was like a fist — *poom!* It knocked me off my feet and chunks of wet clay rained on me. I struggled to sit up.

There was a hole in the trail where Little Monkey had been. A voice screamed from the hole. Then stopped.

25

"Oh God," Amie moans. Her voice is small and her face is pointed to the little fire.

I am staring into my cup. There is a little cold tea in the bottom.

"Don't say any more if you don't want to," Hook says. His voice is thick.

Heather's hands are signing the same thing, but I interrupt. "No, I want to tell you. I want to get it out." I am not crying. I am calm. It's like I'm talking about someone else.

I drink the last drop of tea and balance my cup on one of the gray stones that ring the fire. Then I start to talk again.

I don't remember much about the next few days. When we came down out of the mountains and the jungle we started to travel a little in the daytime. Maybe Father was in a hurry now. Maybe it was because we could travel longer without . . . without Little Monkey.

We reached the flatlands. The rain kept up. For one whole day we crossed grassland. The tall grass was higher than us and the rough blades plucked at our wet clothes. We were numb — cold, worn out, and hungry. Father walked like a dead man. Spring cried constantly.

Sometimes we passed the bodies of soldiers. Some in gray uniforms, some in brown. They were bloated and rotting. A lot of the soldiers were about my age.

When we came near a live village we would sneak around it. But a lot of the villages were dead. They all looked the same — burned huts, bomb holes scattered all around, full of water. Dead animals rotting. And dead people.

Finally we reached Long Bow village on the big river. We had a relative there, a distant cousin. Spring and I hid in the long grass by the river. Father sneaked into the village that night and found Cousin Tran.

For a few days we floated downriver on Cousin Tran's sampan. It was a wide, flat river, I remember. Tea colored, with lumpy purple mountains in the distance. We pretended to be river people. We ran into lots of patrols —Browns near Long Bow village, then Grays when we got closer to the city. The patrols would search all the sampans they found and usually took people's belongings, if they were worth anything.

One night we reached the city. Spring was scared, and so was I, by the huge dark shapes that lined the shore. We had never travelled outside our village. We had never seen buildings more than one story high. We had never seen buildings made of bricks and cement. And so *many* of them!

Cousin Tran steered the sampan to a jetty. I don't know how he found it in the dark. We threw our bundles up onto the jetty and scrambled out. We hurried so Cousin Tran could get away. A patrol boat might see him.

We whispered goodbyes and thank yous. His sampan backed away, then swung into the current, facing upriver. We could barely see him bending and rising as he pushed the single oar against the water.

Spring and I followed Father, holding the rope. The dark streets were almost empty. He seemed to know where he was going. We hid when we heard footsteps or motors. We walked for hours. It was scarier than the jungle.

Father hid Spring and me in a big warehouse. Then he left us, saying he would be back as soon as he could. But he might be gone a long time. We were terrified. We crouched in the dark, surrounded by bad smells.

"How about some fresh tea, George?" Amie's voice.

The sun is high and the campsite is hot. Hook has taken his T-shirt off but he is still wearing long pants. Heather and Amie are wearing bathing suits. They must have had them on under their clothes. Heather's freckles are bright in the sun.

I hold my cup out for more tea, pushing it against Amie's hand. She holds the cup with her thumb hooked inside. She carefully sets the pot's spout on the cup's lip and pours slowly. When the tea in the cup touches her thumb she stops pouring. She hands back the cup.

White smoke climbs straight up from the little flames. I blow on the tea, then sip. A fat hornet buzzes down to sit on a rock beside the fire. It walks in circles for a bit, then floats up and away.

The lake is a flat, hard blue. The islands look like green stones scattered on a blue table.

"Do you remember the name of the city?" Heather's hands ask.

After I pass this on I answer. "No. I think Father had been there before. Spring and I hadn't. I . . . I think it's where Father took my mother when she got the sickness. She never came back."

After a minute Amie asks, "How come it was so dark there? No streetlights like we have?"

"I know," Hook cuts in. "Blackout. So the bombers can't see their targets."

"Oh, yeah," Amie says. "That makes sense. Why didn't I think of that?"

"Cause you don't have Siggy here, that's why," Hook laughs. His laugh is weak and doesn't come out right. "Everybody knows you're really a bean-brain and it's Siggy that does all your thinking."

Amie sticks her tongue out at him.

Heather starts to sign. "Your memory's working like crazy now, isn't it George? You're telling what happened as if you were reading it from a book."

I am quiet after I pass this on.

Hook peels the wet bark from a couple of sticks and feeds the fire.

"Maybe," he says quietly, "having a good memory isn't such a hot thing after all." He looks at Heather, then Amie, then me.

I know I can't explain it to them yet. But I feel like every word of the story is a weight falling off me.

I don't know how long Father left us in the warehouse. But I remember the day we went to the harbor. It was a very hot morning and the sun was fierce. Our clothes were clean and we had fresh food in our bundles. Each of us had a boat ticket and special papers with black writing and red stamps all over them. The papers were wrapped in clear plastic envelopes hung with string from our necks. I don't know where Father got them.

The harbor was very busy — lots of ships tied to the docks and wagons and pushcarts rumbling around. As we walked along, soldiers — Grays — would stop us and ask Father questions. They were always rude and mean but Father answered in a calm, polite voice. Father had warned Spring and me not to talk unless we had to. We were pretending to be from a Gray village on the north edge of the city. Father thought White Crane village might be controlled by Browns by then. He didn't want to take any chances.

Finally Father found the ship he was looking for. We stopped and looked at it. It was old. It seemed to sag in the brown water. Scaly red rust covered it from the front to the back. It was already crowded, but people were walking up a long wood ramp to get on.

But first they had to pass the Grays at the foot of the ramp. There were five of them. One sat behind a little wooden table. The rest stood behind the table, smoking and talking.

We walked up to them. I was scared. I held Spring's trembling hand.

The soldiers who were standing looked bored. Their uniforms were messy and stained. They leaned on their rifles. But the fat one behind the table had on a new uniform. He had it buttoned up tight, so the collar forced a roll of fat up under his chin. He ordered us to hand over our papers, then tore them from the plastic cases.

I could feel Spring shaking. I turned and hugged her, trying to make her calm. Behind me, I knew Father was having trouble. I think it was because Father was born in China, so his papers were different. The fat soldier would snap a question at him and Father would talk in his calm, even voice. I turned to watch.

The soldier held our papers in his sweaty hands. He

would look at me, then at Spring. There was a line-up of people behind us now.

The soldier stamped one set of papers and handed them to Father. He put them back in the case and hung it around Spring's neck.

More talk. The four Grays leaned on their rifles, looking bored. The sun beat down on us. Stamp. Another set of papers was tossed at Father and he gave them to me.

More talk. Father's voice, calm and even. The fat Gray's voice, cruel and angry. I did not understand. If he hated Father he should be glad to let him leave.

Father took a bundle of paper money from his pocket. He laid it on the table, talking quietly. The four standing Grays laughed. The fat soldier laughed.

Stamp.

We hurried up the ramp and onto the ship.

When we had found a clear spot on the packed deck, we settled down. "Keep these things for me," Father said, handing me all the money he had left and a paper with writing and official stamps on it.

"And take good care of Spring," he added, "in case anything happens to me."

That scared me more than anything so far. Before I could ask him why he had given me the papers and money Spring asked, "Where are we going, Father?"

He said he didn't know. "Wherever they will take us in," he said. His voice was tense.

I asked him why the soldiers gave us so much trouble.

He spat over the rail into the dirty brown water. "With soldiers there is always trouble. They eat trouble like rats eat garbage. It's how they live. Those Grays said I might be a spy. It's ridiculous." He spat again. "Look at these poor, miserable people around us. Forced to run away from their homes so these ridiculous puppets in their gray and brown suits can play their political games and fight their civil wars. This is *our* country, but we are treated like enemies."

Spring began to cry. "I wish Little Monkey were with us."

Father stopped talking and we tried to get Spring to go to sleep. After a while I lay down, too, and went to sleep.

I woke up when I heard shouting. It was almost dark on the ship. I looked up and saw Father standing between two soldiers. They had short guns hanging from shoulder straps, pointed at him. They kept jabbing him with the points and yelling. He was trying to talk to them. One of them swung his gun, smashing the handle into Father's face. Father fell over Spring's legs.

Spring woke up, saw him, and started to wail. Father struggled to his feet. Blood poured from his mouth. Spring stood and ran to him, wrapping her arms around his legs. The Gray who had hit Father pushed her away. Then the two Grays jabbed him some more, trying to get him to move.

"Don't worry," he called as they shoved him toward the ramp. "I'll be back."

The next morning the men who worked the ship started to get ready to leave.

I was going crazy. I wanted to run down the ramp and search for Father. But where would I go? How would I find him? What would happen to Spring while I searched for him? I felt like a piece of rice paper ripped in half. One part wanted to go find Father. The other wanted to follow his command to take care of Spring. It was my duty to look after her now.

So I stayed.

I am crying. The sobs tear at my chest. Tears stream down. It's like I am having The Dream, but I'm awake. I can hear the birds and the fire. I can see my three friends, blurred with tears. I want to die.

Finally I can talk again. "You know what happened after that."

"The storm," Hook says quietly.

I nod, wiping tears away. "The ship went into many ports, but they all turned us away. They called us 'Boat People.' Then I heard people on the deck saying 'Hong Kong' over and over. I never heard of that place. But those people never made it to Hong Kong."

I look down into my empty cup. "I didn't deserve to live. I should have died, too. I'm ashamed to be alive."

The crying controls me. I sit hunched over, wiping the tears. Again and again. But they won't stop.

I notice Hook lower himself from his log and lever himself away from the fire. I feel someone move beside me, take my hand, hold it tight. Amie. Someone else puts an arm around my shoulder. Heather.

"I should have died. It's my fault," a voice chants. My voice.

Hook appears again on the other side of the fire. "Hey, George Horse." His voice is firm, strong. "Look."

I can't look into his face.

"Look!" he says again.

I look up, wiping the tears away again. Hook tosses something into my lap. Something soft.

It's a sock. A white one, with blue trim.

26

I still have the sock in my hand as I shove Hook's chair across the road toward the beach. The trees throw long shadows across the road, like bars, but the beach is blazing with bright light. The wheels sink into the hot sand and the chair stops. I squat in front of Hook and he climbs onto my back.

He is silent as I carry him to the edge of the water where the sand is dark and cool. I crouch again and Hook slides off. He is wearing his bathing suit. His skinny white legs stick straight out in front of him. He turns himself around and levers himself into the water, waist deep. There are two wobbly grooves in the sand where his heels dragged.

I sit cross-legged at the edge of the water, letting the tiny waves lap at my knees and feet. I stare at the sock, twisting it in my hands. I know what it means. It means Hook wants me to be strong, like that cripple in the race.

I stopped crying a minute ago, before we came down to

the water, long after Heather and Amie crept quietly away from the fire and headed for the lake. I can see their heads farther out in the lake, as if they are floating on the water. Amie is humming, and her voice hangs over the water like smoke.

I feel ashamed because I cried so much. I feel small. The crying took me over, tearing sobs from deep down inside me. I lost face.

"What did you say, George?"

I realize I was talking out loud. "I said I lost face, Hook."

A smile gleams on his face, then disappears. He was going to make a joke, but he changed his mind.

"What do you mean?"

"It means . . . I shamed myself. Because I cried so much."

"Come on, George, we're *friends* here. You know better than that. Forget it."

He lies back so his face is pointed to the clear sky, squinting. Then he lets himself sink below the surface of the lake. After a few seconds he comes up, blowing and puffing. Farther out, the two heads turn. Heather's face shows very white, Amie's black.

I look down again, twisting at the sock. My two sisters' faces creep into my mind. Spring's long black braids. Little Monkey's grin. I can feel my throat thicken again. I cough to cover up, so I won't cry again. I squeeze my eyes shut.

"Let it go, George," Hook says softly. "It's okay."

But his words save me and the wave passes. I take a deep breath.

"Hook, I can't do it."

"You can't do what?"

I hold up the sock. "I can't be like that guy you told me about. The guy with the metal leg who ran in the marathon race. He was a hero. He was strong inside, like you."

I drop the sock onto the hot sand. "I'm not like that. I never *will* be."

Hook lies back in the water and lets himself sink again. Up in the sky, a white bird is floating above the lake, like a snowflake that won't fall.

Hook comes up. He wipes his face with his hand, runs his fingers through his curly black hair. He looks straight at me.

"You're tougher than the three of us put together, George Horse."

"No, I'm *not*!" I almost shout the words. "I'm *not* strong. Hook, I'm afraid to go to sleep tonight. I'm terrified that I'll have The Dream again. That's not being strong!"

"Yeah, well, maybe you will. But the thing about nightmares is, sooner or later you wake up, right? No matter how bad it gets, you come back. And when you do, Amie, Heather, and I will be there."

Hook cups water in his hand and splashes it over his thick arm and chest. His muscles flex under the skin.

"I wish I was dead."

"Dammit, George, cut the crap!" Hook's arm explodes from the water and he jerks his thumb back over his shoulder. His words are like stones. "You think those two out there haven't thought the same thing *lots* of times? You think all of us haven't spent a lot of time crying like you did today?"

He takes a long breath and blows it out slowly. He talks again, but his words are soft now. "Listen, ol' buddy, I'm not going to tell you I know how you feel, because I don't. Nobody does. But your dad and your sisters didn't go through all that hell so you could come to Canada and give up on yourself."

I look at him there, waist deep in the water. His legs are like white tubes. The wavelets move them under the water. The legs disappear into the green shorts with the leaping red frogs on them. Above the shorts, Hook is big, with a thick, tanned chest and wide shoulders. His hook is off and the scar on his stump shows up white against his tan. Hook is weak and strong at the same time.

So is Amie. She is blind, but she is really smart. Heather is a deaf-mute but she is smart, too, and she always knows how people feel. All three of them are strong in spirit. I wish my spirit was strong, too, but it isn't. That's the reason I'm a cripple.

Hook's voice breaks in on my thoughts. "Hey, George, how about doing me a favor?"

"Okay."

"How about showing me that new *Shàolín* Form I've seen you practicing lately?"

I don't really want to but I get up and walk a few steps away from the water where the ground is fairly flat. The sand is hot on my bare feet. I turn and face the lake. Heather and Amie are out there silent and still. I take a deep breath and try to clear my mind.

"Put the sock on, George."

I do as he says, pulling the white sock on tight. I compose myself again, feet together, hands at my sides, eyes looking out over the calm blue water, focused on a point in the clear sky above Sugarloaf Island.

Moving slowly and smoothly I begin the Form, stepping, blocking, punching. The Forms are like fighting an invisible opponent. All the movements are planned and you have to memorize them and practice until you do them perfectly. This Form is a black belt Form that I started to learn a few weeks ago. It's long, with lots of hard movements.

I finish the Form but start it again right away. I made

too many mistakes the first time through. My mind is getting clear. I can feel strength coming. I can feel the sun hot on my body, the bright sand hot on my bare foot. Sweat trickles down to the waistband of my shorts and drips from my nose. It stings my eyes. My blocks and punches are powerful. When I kick, sand flies. Each time I punch or kick I yell *Hài!*

I finish the Form. Start again. Gliding, whirling, striking, shouting. It's like a dance. I am dancing on the hot sand at the edge of the water.

CANADIAN TITLES FROM GENERAL PAPERBACKS

Picture Books, Ages 4 - 6

The Picnic	Kady Macdonald Denton	340-494352
Twelve Dancing Princesses	Janet Lunn & Lazlo Gal	458-985406

Fiction & Non-Fiction, Ages 7 - 9

David Suzuki Asks: Did You Know About Light & Sight	Peter Cook & Laura Suzuki	7736-72451
David Suzuki Asks: Did You Know About Insides & Outsides	Peter Cook & Laura Suzuki	7736-72877
The Lady of Strawberries	Helen Chetin & Anita Kunz	7725-90133
Beckoning Lights	Monica Hughes	7736-7280X
Gold Fever Trail	Monica Hughes	7736-72796
Treasure of the Long Sault	Monica Hughes	7736-7277X
A Very Small Rebellion	Jan Truss	7736-72788

Fiction, Ages 9 - 11

Not Impossible Summer	Sue Ann Alderson	7736-72869
Old Coach Road	Wilma Alexander	7736-73059
Queen's Silver	Wilma Alexander	7736-72850
Stampede	Mary Blakeslee	7172-25801
Mysterious Mr. Moon	Anne Stephenson	7736-72842
Lost Treasure of Casa Loma	Eric Wilson	7736-7165X
Terror in Winnipeg	Eric Wilson	7736-71641

Young Adult, Ages 12 & Up

Chapter One	Sue Ann Alderson	7736-72834
Absolutely Invincible!	William Bell	7736-72915
Crabbe	William Bell	7736-7232X
Brothers and Strangers	Marilyn Halvorson	7737-53699
Dare	Marilyn Halvorson	7736-72672
Dreamspeaker	Cam Hubert	7736-72303
Dream Catcher	Monica Hughes	416-052029
Ghost Dance Caper	Monica Hughes	458-802409
Hunter in the Dark	Monica Hughes	7736-72273
Sandwriter	Monica Hughes	416-955207
Far From Shore	Kevin Major	7737-54288
Hold Fast	Kevin Major	7737-54296
Sixteen is Spelled O - U - C - H	Joan Weir	7736-72907